IRONBARK

Jay Carmichael is a writer and editor. His first novel, *Ironbark*, was shortlisted for the 2016 Victorian Premier's Award for an Unpublished Manuscript. His writing has been published by beyondblue and appeared widely in print and online, including in *Overland*, *The Guardian*, and *SBS*. Jay lives and works in Melbourne.

IRONBARK

Jay Carmichael

SCRIBE

Melbourne • London

Scribe Publications
18–20 Edward St, Brunswick, Victoria 3056, Australia
2 John St, Clerkenwell, London, WC1N 2ES,
United Kingdom

First published by Scribe 2018

Typeset in Adobe Caslon Pro by the publishers

Printed and bound in Australia by Griffin Press

 The paper this book is printed on is certified
against the Forest Stewardship Council®
Standards. Griffin Press holds FSC chain of
custody certification SGS-COC-005088. FSC
promotes environmentally responsible, socially
beneficial and economically viable management
of the world's forests.

9781925322552 (Australian edition)
9781925548907 (ebook)

A CiP record for this title is available from the National
Library of Australia.

scribepublications.com.au
scribepublications.co.uk

For Guy

Two weeks after

Markus is shoeless. He burnt his pairs on a bonfire held beside the house about two weeks ago. Shoes make no difference. He looks through the lace draped across the inside of his bedroom window. It's lunchtime. He's naked and yet to shower. He yawns and scratches his balls, akin to stretching out your muscles after a slept-like-a-log night. The sun fails to break open the thin film of clouds. Since that storm, the rain withholds itself and everything is preserved, overcast. Inanimate things breathe, and some mornings he's been stunned by this apparent breathing. Everything around him is living, and he's stagnant because of the knot in his belly.

One of the flat northern plains is covered by knee-high grey-green grass. Murky violet sways between its tufts.

There're no persons or animals, and there are no fences or houses or trees. This Plain takes a day's travel from one side to the other, and if you make the journey to its edge, you'll find the Hills, which bear on their backs eucalypts (various) and grevillea (family *Proteaceae*). From the middle of the Plain this hilly edge is unseeable, because at its centre is the Plain's only imperfection.

The grass grows to the imperfection's edge and no further. At this edge, the ground falls down sharp cliffs to form the Depression: a gaping, deep gash in the otherwise perfect surface. The Depression, bound by these unscaleable cliffs, is a smaller area set one hundred and fifty metres below the level of the Plain. Here there are farms and fences, properties and people, sheep runs and dairies, furrows for wheat and rye and barley and canola and maize and corn, orchards and vegetables. Wind dances in the grassy paddocks and screeching sulphur-crested cockatoos (*Cacatua galerita*) frequent the area. In the centre of the Depression is the township of Narioka (aka Noaks).

A hundred people live in Narioka, with a further hundred producers living on the farms and properties spreading outward to the cliffs. This is enough to make do. Other than this binding rock-face, there's an ephemeral lake on the outskirts of town with a tributary creek, also empty, cutting through town. The Lake has a natural ironbark (*Eucalyptus sideroxylon*) bushland around its edges. They say you're lucky to see either lake or creek fill in your lifetime.

Thirteen days after the destructive thunderstorm, the *Narioka Leader* is folded over a dining table chair. Markus Bello looks at its front page, which has a story on the progress of the railway to the city. It says they have surveyed the valuable space — 'valuable' because there's only so much land they can acquire from the Depression without affecting the producers. The final paragraph mentions that the recent storm, and the record-breaking rain it dumped, may cause delays. This same rain, even though it's winter, will not have broken the drought.

The master bedroom door opens behind him. A warm hand touches his shoulder. Elba: his to-be stepmother. She keeps walking, her fingers sliding across his shoulder blades until there's no more of him for her to touch. They coexist. She re-boils the kettle. She prepares a tea and when she sits across from him, he smells chamomile. She's sitting side-on, and this pose allows her to rest her left elbow on top of the chair, hand under chin. She gazes out the glass sliding door behind the table and runs her fingers through her long hair. Outside, her to-be husband, and Markus's father, tends to pumpkins in one of his veggie patches. Elba asks Markus when the overcast will clear. He watches her pick up her tea with both hands and blow across the peachy surface. He scans the *Leader* for the weather report. She puts the teacup down. He stops at a random page of the paper and points to a random illustration. He needs hope as much as she does.

He says, as Cat jumps up onto the table, There's a story about the weather. Cat sits for a bit, sanctioning Elba's strokes under its chin and behind its ears. It stands and stretches and walks to Markus, where it rolls down over the paper. Elba resumes her initial pose. Each of the previous thirteen days has felt like a late-arvo soapie; a little bold, a little beautiful.

Markus walks into the bathroom and turns the heat lamp on high. Soon its strength pricks into the back of his neck. He assesses his shoulder in the mirror. A large bruise the colour of bile wraps itself over his pectoral muscle and collarbone, down his right arm, and stops above the wrist.

His phone rings beside him. No Caller ID.

For thirteen days — those bloody thirteen days — he's been flicking through his past to find a point of reference. He hadn't yet caught on anything, until now, until this: Georges's phone call. He sees Georges and Grayson in the same place. They appear to him as markers of faith amongst a crowd of hundreds of others from around Narioka. These others surround them, but to Markus, they fall far short.

On the other end of the phone, Georges clears his throat. He could be at a café, for there's the tink of metal on china and the hush of traffic. Georges has put a bookmark in between the pages containing Narioka and the pages of his success as an emerging artist. Which is, in part, why Markus agrees to meet Georges at the pub in Noaks later that afternoon; the conversation is over before he can take any of it back. He spends most of the arvo lag looking into the pantry. He doesn't want to eat, necessarily, but a hunger of a different kind is growing in his stomach and can't be satiated with chips or bikkies: Markus wants to redeem a part of his past, and it's Georges who's to be consumed to satisfy this unsteady need. Or so he hopes.

With half a pot warming in his rough hands, Markus waits for Georges. The bar bench is sticky on his forearms. Sweat forms in the space where his bare feet touch the barstool. The fire in here's too hot. There's no one else except the bartender. Markus avoids eye contact.

The bartender says something about being a brute. Yer can't trust what the paper says.

Markus looks up at him. Molten lava bulges in his throat; his face may begin to melt. He says nothing, which doesn't matter because Georges comes in. Markus turns to greet him.

Georges is straight from the turn of the century: distressed jeans, tight, knees torn out, thighs threadbare, the cuffs hanging down the backs of his dusty Volleys, which are scuffed. Markus stops himself from checking to see if there's a hole in the denim showing off the undies Georges may be wearing. Faux-silk boxers, Marvel-patterned, perhaps? No. Though there's pattern here: a patchwork of red, grey, and black intersecting in the flannelette long-sleeve, buttons undone, hanging over Georges's slim frame. Underneath, a white singlet.

Nice, says Markus. He'd forgotten that Georges's gaze is almost ceremonious: eyes like the blue light coming through stained glass and shining into a phial of holy water.

Georges is looking at Markus's feet. Least I'm fully dressed, he says. Where are your shoes at?

Markus fills his mouth with beer.

If you tried to get round like that in the city, says Georges, you'd get a syringe in the bottom of your foot. A laugh. A smile. The gap since the last time they spoke closes, a tiny bit.

They sit beside each other, exchanging little.

How's the city? says Markus.

Busy. Georges puffs out his chest.

Still living with your mum down there?

Georges nods.

Must be different to ol' Noaks here.

Sure is, says Georges. He sucks in a draught of his own.

Most of the boys at high school used to call Georges *dirty sanchez*. Markus had had to Google what it means:

after anal, you pull out and wipe your bare dick across your partner's lip, forming a faecal moustache. At the time, the unknown meaning of dirty sanchez, the implication of 'dirty', had been enough for Georges to be undesired, to be tainted.

Markus wants to say sorry. Doesn't.

It's been too long, he says.

Georges's fingers swirl in the condensation on the side of his pot. Things get in the way.

But with phones and stuff — two people shouldn't stop talking. Markus coughs, brings his chin to his chest, and then sips his beer to clear his throat. Georges pats him once, hard, on the shoulder, his healing, bruised shoulder. It doesn't hurt as much as bring Markus comfort, for some bizarre reason.

C'mon, Georges says as he gets off his stool. Enough of that. He's at the jukebox, and in minutes a Kanye and Jay-Z song plays. 'Otis'. Markus spills his beer as he turns on his stool to face Georges.

They're not going to talk about what's brought Georges back to Narioka, which is why if he were drunker, Markus'd smash the glass pot on his own face to cover what he begins to notice. It's an urge towards Georges, as if to pick him up. To take them both away from here. Narioka. Or even to crawl up Georges's body and pitch a tent inside his heart. He watches Georges dancing as if he knows how to dance. Dirty sanchez.

At the end of the song, Georges skols and says, Time for me to go. Early start back to the city.

Markus says, You got a place to stay?

Kinda.

What's that mean?

Well, I—

Nah, Markus swats the answer away with his hands. He says, Come to mine. Ren won't mind. And before Georges can answer, Markus is up and out the door.

Outside the pub, Markus shivers. The night is silent and silky-black. The streetlight orange and hazy in the fog. When Markus breathes out, a white plume coils from his lips. The scene spins, repeats, back and forth. Fark it's nippy, he says.

Georges laughs as if trying to puff away dust that's rested on the tip of his nose. Markus bites his tongue because Grayson used to do that. Georges's voice, whatever he's saying — maybe something about the cold — stops Markus from speaking, from acting.

The young men walk back to Markus's father's farm with the silence from the paddocks wedging between them as they go into the darkness. Markus blames the drink for not making small talk — he'll probably slur his words — though it's more that his redemption never came. Redemption he wanted for all the lost years, for all the things unsaid and those he witnessed being said but never stopped those boys from saying. And now, still walking, the crushed stone soft-crunching, Markus fills with confusion about what it is he wants.

Once inside the old farmhouse, Georges says, I'll sleep on the couch.

Nah, man. Markus makes up an excuse that Cat will piss him off. It's better in my room, he says, we can top-and-tail if you want. Georges scoffs at this, so the young men sleep side by side: Georges on top of the covers and Markus underneath. In the morning, Markus wakes with his head on Georges's chest. Georges isn't awake and Markus needs to shit. He slips from bed, from the room, and to the toilet. No one else is up. When he returns and finds Georges sat up on the side of the bed, putting on his shoes, Markus says, You off?

Georges nods.

Will you be back?

Georges shrugs. He stands up and puts his hands in his jeans' pockets. Dunno, Mark. He smiles tight. Dunno if I wanna come back to this shithole. He laughs.

And so does Markus, but when he crosses his arms over his chest the laugh cuts short. He says, You need a ride back into town?

Nah, the walk'll clear my head.

Afterward, Markus returns to his bedroom's window, hiding behind the lace like an introverted pervert. Georges disappears down the drive. Outside, a bead of dew falling from the eave lands on the petal of an orange geranium flower with such force that the flower's stem bends, as if bowing, to release itself of the drop. Once released it flicks back to stillness.

Sometimes Markus likes the night, and sometimes he wishes he could sleep right through, undisturbed, from the moment of last light to the moment of first. Other times he wishes light didn't exist.

His clock radio flashes an angry, red 3.59am. His father, Rene, will be up soon, and Elba: for work, for passing time. Markus goes by the weak moonlight filtering through the skylight in the hallway, walks past the kitchen/dining room and into the lounge room.

Snake is Rene's pet carpet python (*Morelia spilota*). Coiled in the sand at the corner of its glass tank, which his father displays in the lounge, it looks like a tiger snake (*Notechis scutatus*) in the dim light. It's passive now, facing its abysmal eyes outward, unmoving. Markus hasn't had to feed it in a while. When he did have to, Snake, coiled as it is now, would eye the shaking rodents and, without warning, Snake's slim body would pounce, mouth agape, spiny teeth bared. Snake would make a dull thud when it struck, and the mouse would declare a dying squeak as it was squeezed dead.

Markus moves across to, and bends beside, the fireplace and opens its door. Inside, he builds a loose tepee of kindling and puts scrunched-up balls of newspaper underneath. He lights the paper and watches as it burns against the wood. Mute orange flames behind the dirty glass wobble like liquid. Markus wishes he'd fall into those flames and drift away on the log burning beneath. He pulls the blanket from the couch, lies down in front of the fire. The glow sways over the floor in front of him.

Later that week he walks barefoot into town, allowing himself to unwind with the sandy track through the fields and across the bridge over the empty creek.

A little away from the road and outside the township, bulldozers and rollers and other brutish things stand sleepy at the site chosen for the future Narioka Station. The metallic beasts guard the site manager's office.

Markus finds himself not at the shoe store but at the brim of town and, a little further, the library. Ananke, the librarian, has crisscrossed the carpet with cold steel shelves. The aisles are quiet. He pulls three books: a Thomas, a Byron, and *Maurice*. He puts the Forster on the bottom and grabs a fourth paperback, a collection by Dorothy Porter. At the service desk, Ananke scans two, and then, at the third, halts. *Maurice*. The words rush by Ananke's soft-skinned fingers, flipping the pages. Ananke smiles lightly and places the books in a calico bag, saying to keep them an extra week.

Markus walks down the main street. Georges is right: shoes are a necessity. Though Georges hadn't said, it'd been in the way he'd looked at Markus. Markus follows the ancient scratching in the main drag's pavement, and the flat black circles of discarded gum.

Melville Street glimmers in daylight. Both the street itself and the people who walk it are unperturbed. As they approach him on the street, he knows they are preparing their piss-weak smiles, preparing to meet his gaze and offer pleasantries. *For your loss*, they might say. He walks with his head down and denies them their self-satisfaction. He walks by the chemist and then to the shoe shop. He doesn't know the assistant inside, and she seems not to know him either because she waits behind the counter. She flicks some paperwork and picks a scabby pimple on her jawline. Close up, she has brown eyes. And where she stands she fills some kind of space, as if a guardian. She points him to a burnt-orange pair of Vans, which he tries on, tying the orange laces tight. Beaming smile. Purchase. He leaves, wearing the Vans and carrying the calico bag of books.

He walks almost three-quarters of the way along Melville Street before turning down Quinn then left on Madigan. The streetscape opens up: on his right the Lake, or rather, what is left of it. Under a eucalypt, he sits by what was once the Lake's edge, maybe three years ago. About that. It had filled, frozen, broken up, and flooded, making Narioka fearful of any water that fell from sky or tap; fearful that things would overflow again. Fuckers. Now, the Lake is an expansive dip in the ground, covered in drying weeds and surrounded by a binding face of ironbarks, which look tired, black, and smug. In the middle of the Lake is a faux island whose tapered end, which you can't see from here, joins onto the time-share Country Club. Along the side of the Lake, two rabbits (feral) scratch the hard dirt and bound about each other, in and out of the sun and shade.

He makes his way back to his father's farm. He finds an empty shoebox under his bed. Small clumps of dust blow away to the windowsill. It's getting on in the late afternoon. He places the library books inside the box and slides it under his bed, hearing it hit the wall at the bedhead.

He's touching the bandage he's kept around his hand, which used to cover the bite Cat had made. He takes it off now because when he pushes against the dirty fabric there's no pain. Underneath, his skin is pale, and the bite's no more than a shiny scar. He decides to wash. The shower's steam makes the white tiles underfoot dissolve into each other. He almost can't see his feet. The smell of the Pears soap calms his belly, his mind. He wipes the amber bar over his body and around his junk. He replaces the soap on its holder, and foams up its residue on his skin. At his cock, he rubs the foam into his pubes, which, along with heat and tranquillity, makes him hard. He soaps his shaft while his other hand touches his scrotum. He closes his eyes ...

Georges grabs him, draws him close, like chest to chest. And there, in between their faces, he hears air whistle through Georges's nostrils. Georges. Markus doesn't want to be let go. He wants the chest, the heartbeat beating against his own. He listens to Georges. Warm. He listens to the air whistling in each of Georges's nostrils again and watches his eyeballs slide from side to side to side to side. Alive. There is a silent moment no longer than a second in which he wants their lips to press hard against each other. Present—

Markus cums. Their lips do not touch.

He knocks his kneecap into the glass shower screen, and that sound — the very disjunction and the little bit of pain in his patella — shatters the imagery.

Rene keeps four hanging baskets along the front veranda. In each he grows a single succulent, which, he could've once told Markus, is called a donkey tail (*Sedum morganianum*). Long lime-green tendrils of clustered claws escape the red dirt their roots are confined to. In a light breeze, even if you just breathe out nearby, these tendrils sway like horizontal ripples on a body of water. Too much. If you pull back on imagination, as Rene does, these hangers are embellishments that take the eye away from flaking weatherboards and a rusting bullnose. The recent storm knocked each of the four hangers down. They've lain smashed and spreadeagled on the brickwork pavement since. Rene's cleaning them this evening. The straw broom brushing outside distracts Markus because its sound mimics that of rain. He rolls over. Breathes in and out of his nose to calm his irritation — well, at least that's what he wants to believe it is. His stomach has begun strangling itself. He slides his window open as Rene scrapes the broom, sweeping the last of the first pot's dirt away. A phone call interrupts Markus: Cecily. Again. He ignores and deletes the message she's left.

It isn't pleasurable for him to wake early. Today, he starts the apprenticeship he was meant to a few weeks back. Dark outside.

His father comes in and turns the light on. Markus covers his face. Rene pulls the doona off. In the kitchen, Rene's made him toast and packed him a lunch box for the day. He hands him a mug of coffee. Markus chews a mess of toast he doesn't want and chases it with the last of the coffee. Rene takes him into town because Markus is bringing his faulty motorbike. At Brute Burrows'

Mechanics, his father helps him heave the metal carcass out of the ute's tray and then heads off. Markus wheels his bike into the garage, stands straight and kicks the bike's stand down.

The garage smells of oil and is cold; it would feel almost clinical if it weren't for the pot-belly fire crackling. Smoky scent fills the room.

Brute holds out his hand.

Markus clears his throat and puts his shoulders back. He shakes with Brute. Not long ago, he'd slung this elephantine body up against the pub's brick wall, because it'd threatened him. That's irrelevant now. Forget it. Markus doesn't need a tour. Brute says, Yer've been here enough with me son that this place should be like a second home.

A few galahs (*Eolophus roseicapillus*) burst out from a stand of thick melaleuca across the road. They chirrup and screak and swoop up and over the garage's entrance.

Brute gets to work on the motorbike. Bent down beside the bike, he sucks his bottom lip. He asks, Who did the shoddy cover-up job?

Buff.

Brute asks for the spanner.

Markus reaches around to the bench behind them, steps a little. His shoe, one of the orange Vans, stubs and his fingertips knock the spanner. It scrapes over the bench's edge, drops. A dull light reflects off it before its head hits the concrete floor. The noise slows, echoing in his mind even after the spanner rests. Markus hands Brute the spanner. Brute discards it and grabs lock-grip pliers instead.

At lunch, Brute says he has to pop down the street. Yer want anythin'?

Markus shows him the lunch Rene made.

Brute sniffs and turns away.

The day continues in a quick rhythm.

Brute says, Yer motorbike won't ever go properly. He's interrupted by an older man dropping his car by, telling them to fix it up quick.

Brute remains silent as a ghoul. A sullen face indicating *leave it with me*, and again to a woman, and again to the youngest Drumanure boy, whose pushbike's spokes are done for. Brute tells Markus to leave at about three o'clock. I'll have a chat this evenin' with Ren, mate.

The land between town and Markus's father's house stretches wide, flat, and forever. And it makes him feel like he's flying upside-down.

The way Brute had held his body when he'd undone and rolled down the top half of his jumpsuit was forceful. It had revealed a grey singlet and, dangling in the low-cut neckline, a gold neck chain with a crucifix attached, which had swung side to side as he moved. Brute's son, Buff, wears one similar. As does Elmyra, Markus's oldest friend, who says she got her crucifix from the two-dollar shop, off a rack that has plastic skull-rings and peace-symbol earrings; says that because she paid no more than half the price of a cup of tea, she may as well've stolen it.

Why's the focus on that gold cross? Some things are better left unsaid, even if they say you can say anything in the confessional. The stained glass, the statues looking down at him when he'd gone to church in primary school: these were enough to make him internalise everything. *I farted on my father's pillow* was always good to tell the priest each Friday. Father'd once said, You'd best get off to the doctor, sort that out. Father's dead now, one of them at least. Markus had gone through the Catholic primary school, and the fates of the other Fathers were and still are irrelevant. Sometimes in the afternoon, when the sky's looking deep, he wishes he could throw a stone right up at it and smash it. Watch the shards of blue fall into the Depression. He'd smashed with rail stones, back whenever it was, the church's stained-glass depiction of Jesus and John. And since then it has pissed him off that from the outside, where he had thrown the stone, he couldn't see how the coloured glass must've fallen on the crimson carpet inside. He keeps walking, hands in his pocket. A throw to smash the heavens now from him would fall away, harmless.

The house is empty. He wakes sometime later to the sound of clanging pots: Elba cooking. His bedroom seems smaller. He could use a rail stone, maybe piff it at the window and let the twilight in. Rising and no release. Wanting to break. Abstaining.

He can't.

This method he hardly knows.

He takes the needle he's snuck from Elba's sewing kit and places its sharp, thin point against the skin of his leg. On the inside of his thigh, closer to his groin, he begins to move it back and forth. His skin reddens and tears and bleeds. He pushes harder. When the blood beads and wriggles away from the imperfect gash, threatening to drip to the floor, he stops. He pokes the needle into the side of his mattress. He wipes the blood on his finger and licks it off.

In the shower, he lets the hot water stream onto the wound and the stinging makes his leg shake. He clenches into the fading bruise on his bicep. Numbness.

At dinner, with a hand under the table, he touches the covered abrasion on his leg. Pain.

Rene's concerned. That face ya makin'.

Markus nods and says, The potatoes are too hot.

Elba's on the couch, watching *The Great Outdoors*. She says, It's the potatoes' way of telling you not to eat them because they're bad for you. She sighs, as if the world's an irritating speck of dust she's directing away. She becomes Elmyra, whom Markus has suddenly remembered, and whom he silently promises to text.

His promise is intercepted by Rene's wink. His father's

calloused hand slides the latest *Leader*, his thick forefinger points at a headline. There's a charity football match, he says.

The picture his father's pointing at is of Buff in his footy kit, leaning against a goalpost. Markus stuffs a forkful of potato in his mouth, blowing through his open mouth as the heat sears the roof of his mouth.

His father wakes him by torchlight on the weekend. He touches Markus's foot. I need a hand, one a the heifers is calvin', he says.

Markus follows without complaint because his father's eyes are wide.

Out and down a track, he lags behind. When Rene looks back, Markus nods. He's pretending the bucket's thin metal handle in his hand isn't there. It may as well be slicing him open. A clean slice. The cold, the early dawn, the stars out — all that's meant to be romantic. The chain and jack Rene holds clink together in a steady rhythm. The crispness biting the tip of Markus's nose and the lobes of his ears spreads itself out like freezing pools of water. His breath is dark matter drifting through deep space. Rene turns the torch on him and even though Markus squints, he catches the dark matter turn to silver and the silver go white before it disappears again when Rene flicks the beam away. His father pulls out a handkerchief and hands it to him. The material's warm. Markus wipes his nose. He hears a rustling nearby. Rabbits skitter in the reedy wild oats (*Avena fatua*).

When Markus was a boy, the man had taken him hunting, perhaps for distant relatives of these same rabbits. It was at dusk, when the strong, slender animals bounded across wheat-stubbled paddocks. Rene had caught them in the spotlight while Markus stood in the ute's tray.

Have a shot, bud, his father had said, trying to hand him the shotgun.

Markus'd shaken his head at the smooth wood and matte metal shining in front of him.

Rene hadn't wasted any time — he'd aimed at one of the rabbits, which had stopped and perked up to look right at him, and pulled the trigger. A spray of pellets must've caught the rabbit in the head, because its body had flicked backward, spun round, and landed, back legs kicking, on the soil.

This morning, though, his father's occupied with just the opposite: a louder sound follows, hugging the ground. Rene points the torch to where the sound has come from. Markus puts his free hand in the water in the old white horse-feed bucket he's carrying. Some of its contents splash over the edge with the motion. His flesh is too numb to register the temperature. He licks the residue from the tip of his finger. Rene turns left and wades through the wild oats growing beside the track. At the fence line, he turns the torch back on Markus. Rene takes the bucket from him, lifts it over the fence, and sets it down over the other side. He opens a horizontal gap between wires, and once both men are through, Rene locates the cow.

Markus holds the torch.

His father stands behind the prostrate cow, pumping the jack. The chain moves along the rig's pole and away from the cow as it brings out the calf. The mother groans. It's too slow, and the calf's feet are unmoving. Rene huffs and Markus stands near, not knowing what to do. After a few minutes, Rene pulls the black calf away from the mother and begins to wipe the mucous out of its mouth. Markus rests the torch on the ground; its beam partially illuminates the scene. He pulls at his father's shoulder. Rene moves away, and Markus tips the bucket of water over the calf's head. The mother moos and steam comes from her mouth. The calf remains still. Rene grabs the calf's forelegs; Markus grabs the hind. His father looks at the calf's head, at his hands grasping, at Markus's hands around the hind, and then at his son. They lift it into the air and its head is limp over the soil. They begin to swing it back and forth. Mucous dangles from its mouth. They put it down. Red dirt sticks to its body, to its eyelids. Rene wipes mucous from its face, and he strokes his hand along its throat, back and forth, slow and gentle. The calf coughs, shifting the phlegm from its throat. Its eyes open and roll in its head and it makes a guttural sound.

—

Persisting with, starting anew, starting same, forgetting about the wound on his leg, a run perhaps, walk ... Persisting isn't quite the right word; a word, though, suited enough to the way the Depression is drifting around Markus. Persisting isn't about forgetting the scabby-red wound on his thigh or the bruise that's now faded from his shoulder. Telling people that he's persisting masks what drifts inside him. Smoke haze makes the eucalypts grey and half put together. He recalls those damned rabbits by the Lake as he fiddles with the pen in his pocket. Persisting's pooling his thoughts, making them shallow, making them reflect the things above with wavy iridescence. Some 'thing' stronger is breaking through the surface. Yes. There it is, coming in like a hefty breaker: he'd missed the funeral.

Had said to Rene that he could not go. Rene'd tried to push the bedroom door open. Markus had dug his feet into the carpet and pushed back. Because of that sickness growing in his stomach, which he gets most days (today, it is quiet). Gnarled, solid nausea. It had started after the accident — amidst the dark and beneath the cold falling rain — and grown larger and larger until, in the half hour before Grayson was going to be buried, it had incapacitated Markus. Miss it, Rene had said as he'd thumped his fist on the other side of the door, the force of which had made Markus jolt. Markus spied, from the gap in his bedroom curtains, Rene drive away to town, to the funeral. He'd sat down on his bed, again leaving the drapes unopened, the door closed. There, in the dimness, the outside light had been threatening. Thirteen days it took him to open those damned drapes, as violent as tearing paper.

Being in that bedroom or being out here — there's no difference. It isn't the light that's threatening. Absence produces a vacuum so powerful that any words spoken in it are torn apart.

On the afternoons when Markus is alone and not working (though he doubts Brute will want him back), when Rene and Elba are out shopping or dining or at whatever appointment they keep to themselves, he stays to the lounge. He opens up the curtains and lets the sinking sun come in and lay across the floor. He opens the windows even if it's cold, and he gets himself a beer and sits on the carpet with his back against the low windowsill. On such afternoons he reads. Hates that he reads because it seems useless. It calms his mind, though. He reads volumes from the smallish piles of poetry stacked at the foot of his bed. He's read Thomas, Rimbaud, Cummings, Whitman, and Gunn.

But today, on this specific afternoon, with its specific anticipatory silence, he waits for Elmyra. Where is she anyway? Walking about, most likely, in the shops down the street. He knows whatever it is he knows, i.e., she must have ignored his text.

By five-thirty, he's had two beers. He gets another book of poetry from his room, doesn't even check who wrote the stanzas inside. Beer in hand and book in the other, he sits at the window and sips the ale. Putting that aside, he opens the book. *Don Juan*. Longing and distance and death and breathing. Elmyra's reading it, too. He saw a copy of Byron in her bag. Perhaps that's where she is, unweaving rainbows and clipping an angel's wings. No, that's Keats. Too late for Keats: Elmyra is Hermes, threatening to find a nymph and disappear to the woods forever. Or Demeter.

There's a gentle knock at the door.

Elmyra. The wind blows her hair. She's not dressed-up today. She's been dressing as Marilyn Monroe for ages. She stopped when Grayson died. Here, now, there's an occult partition between her current plainness and the times before, when he'd watch her pat her skirt, run her fingers through her Monroe fringe, glide pink wax over her lips, and pencil black near her eyes.

He says, You aren't Marilyn.

She doesn't answer.

I love Marilyn, he says.

That's why, she says. She's like a speck caught in a shaft of sunlight, suspended in the atmosphere, shifting side to side, floating into view, out of view. She's never in the centre long enough to see her from every angle.

She asks for beer.

He nods.

She removes her shoes and places them inside the door. She walks toward the hall and turns in the direction of his room.

He skids on his socks at her and takes hold of her arm, turns her to the open-plan area.

She looks that way, then back to him. Says, Okay, and walks to get a beer. At the bench, she twists the cap of a Dry. In her black woollen trench coat, with her dark hair, she is beautiful. Where Marilyn gives him confidence and makes him safe, Elmyra as she is challenges him to confront what is between them. Marilyn's like playing games; Elmyra's like playing at life. He doesn't confront it, though. She swigs and turns to him, saying, They're fucked without you.

He raises an eyebrow.

The footy team for the charity match.

Burrows will have it.

Buff? She laughs. Buff Burrows has the least idea of anyone — remember when he first joined and thought wings were still needed?

I trust him.

You say that about everyone.

People are good.

She shakes her head. Only my mother would say that.

That mythical mother, Mrs Robinson: in bed with the blinds drawn and the window open. He'd followed Elmyra in once to see her so-called crazy mother. A summer breeze had made the plastic blinds clack against the window's frame. Mrs Robinson was unmoving, except for her chest rising and falling under the golden sheet, her eyes on him while he'd looked at her forehead and her damp hair hanging over the side of the bed.

Markus hates that of all the rules he tries to live by, this one, believing in the inherent goodness in people, is the one he cannot break.

Buff wouldn't know the word 'charity' if you showed it to him in the dictionary, Elmyra says.

Something must be wrong with him.

Elmyra leans against the kitchen bench. She looks defeated.

Markus walks into the lounge to his beer, which is where he left it, sitting on the carpet in the sunlight.

Elmyra, who has followed him, sinks into the couch.

He sits back where he began, spine turned against the window. He watches her.

She looks at the roof and drinks.

Why did you give up Marilyn?

She scoffs. I didn't give her up.

You're not dressing as her.

She sighs. Says, It seems like too much effort, all things considered. By *all things* she could mean anything:

her mother, Grayson, Burrows, himself.

What's Buff reckon?

He didn't say anything. She wiggles in the couch. He just helped me pack away Marilyn's things.

I could've helped with that.

I know, she says, but you've got your own shit happening. And anyway, she takes a mouthful of beer, Buff's so … immovable. He takes everything I throw at him. No questions.

Elmyra believes she's right when she says Buff's immovable. No questions. But she can't feel what moves boys when they're undressing beside each other in a stuffy change room.

It had happened in PE class. Individual Activities: Grayson, Markus, Buff, and about five or six other boys, all at different stages of puberty, each one of them self-conscious, anxious, and shouting as they walked down Melville Street, sweating under the bitch of burning sun. Subconsciously aware of all that skin around them, beside them. That week they were doing water aerobics at the local outdoor swimming pool. Teacher said to shower in the change rooms before getting in the pool.

The change rooms at the pool had hot, moist concrete underfoot, no roof overhead, and a weathered wooden bench running down the middle. Only two showers at the back. The first two boys ran to get out of the sun and under the shower, to feel a cool rush of water before being allowed out into the big pool. The other boys, including Markus, Buff, and Gray, dropped their bags along the wooden bench and began to get changed.

Most of them wore their togs under their uniform — or, on that particular day, as uniform — but one of the boys got completely starkers. Another boy slapped him on the arse with the back of his hand, saying something like, Geez, yer'd blind us with yer skin if it was any whiter.

Fuck off cunt, said the naked one, least it'd stop yer from checking out me arse.

Not me yer needa worry about, the slapper said, and he seemed to wink and nod, briefly, in Markus's direction. Equally, he could've been flicking a lock of his long, greasy hair from his eyes.

What's that mean? Gray said. He hitched down his school shorts to reveal bright-yellow board shorts.

The slapper flicked his head round again. None yer fucken business, mate.

I'm not yer mate, mate, Gray returned. He took off his shirt.

Too fucken right, said the slapper. He stood up and took off his shirt, too.

Out of nowhere, Buff laughed, loud and short, as he pulled up beside the boys and took a seat in between the slapper and Grayson. He said, Sometimes in the footy showers, yer get these queer fucks looking sideways at yer wang.

Yer'd lap that shit up, Burrows, said the naked boy, who was now in his own pair of board shorts. Tattered at the waistline, faded blue to violet down the sides.

Nah fuck off, said Buff, it makes me all weird. He mock-shivered. I don't know whether to shove me cock down his throat or smash his pimply fucken face in.

Why the fuck would yer want him to suck yer off? the slapper said in all seriousness, the faux-credulity with which he'd initially addressed Buff gone.

Buff shrugged and stood. He grabbed his crotch. Free blowie in the shower block, mate, he said. Just close me eyes — and he did, right there in the middle of the open-roofed change room, with his hands now behind his head and his groin pointed out — and picture Elmyra between me legs.

Markus says now, No questions?

Elmyra shrugs.

And you like that? Markus drinks the amber, warm, and finds it pleasant.

She concedes, finishes her stubby, and gets them both another. She peels the beer bottle's label. Yes, it would be easier if he played along, but their conversation has little life, or at least none that either wishes to acknowledge, and they finish off these beers. The sun has gone. Elmyra lights a candle because, she says, The label says Honeysuckle & Lemon Myrtle. She's started listening to Cold War Kids on repeat. The smell, she says, honeysuckle and lemon myrtle, reminds me of them.

How so?

She sits the candle on the coffee table. The flame casts long shadows over *Juan* and over her — both now far across the room, in the dimness. She says, I've been listening to the one song, over and over on repeat.

What's that?

She hums a melody. Asks, Has Cecily got a hold of you? She's been trying to call.

He says, as he's getting up, Not heard a word.

Hmm, strange. She swears she has.

I bet, he says. He gets, from his bedroom wardrobe, the bottle of absinthe Rene gave him for his eighteenth and which he'd wanted to share with Grayson. The green liquid goes opaque when he adds iced water to it, and she says, It looks like mucous. By the second, they're drinking the firewater (she says, Is this lighter fluid?) straight from shot glasses.

Halfway through her second, Elmyra says, Drinking this makes my throat peel. And as if the layer the liquid has softened her, she says, I miss Grayson — his smile and his laugh.

Markus tilts his head. He intends it to prompt her to explain herself, and to make him believe her.

She doesn't see. She sips her shot and takes the glass from her lips, where it hovers. She leans its rim back to her mouth and pours more of its contents down her throat. She takes it away before it's all gone.

Markus thinks that by focussing on a single part, you might lose the overall hang of Grayson, so he says, I miss *him*.

Her head rolls over the pillow and looks across to Markus.

Markus runs his finger around the rim of the shot glass; his finger slips in. He licks the absinthe from it. Georges said we shouldn't speak of him in the past tense.

But Grayson is gone, Markie. Elmyra downs the small pool of liquid left in her shot. Pours herself another.

Markus doesn't want to drink the remaining absinthe in his glass. Grayson's a part of our existence, he says.

You've had too much, she says.

Do you remember the first time you met him?

She shakes her head. You?

He says, Yes. At that drought fundraiser in the skate park — he got up, remember, and sang. Markus closes his eyes and arches his head back, as if floating on top of unseen water.

They finish their drinks and leave the candle going.

Elmyra says, I need a moment.

Markus goes into his room, strips naked, and then puts a pair of red undies on. He's struggling to get his legs into a pair of blue chequered PJ pants.

She comes in. Pushes him on the bed and pulls the pants on for him before falling into place beside him.

He rests his head on the pillow, and its cool cotton

soothes his burning cheek. He closes his eyes as the mattress beneath him shifts, rocks a little like the ripples made in a puddle. She moves behind him, curls her body into his shape. Her arm around his waist. She touches her nose into the nape of his neck and breathes out down his back. Her leg weaves through his and her toes rest by his. She wriggles them. She pulls the blanket over them, right up to their necks, and pats it flat. She replaces her arm over his waist and hugs him.

What would they say if they could see us now?

She lowers her voice to mock those boys, and says, Give her a squeeze for me.

Markus's laugh bubbles over.

I never took what they said seriously. We knew what was what.

And what was that?

I have no idea, she whispers slowly. But they don't need to know that.

When he wakes next, the moon's lit the room. Elmyra's staring at the roof.

Hi.

Her head lolls to him, her lips kiss the tip of his nose. She says, What's the roof made of?

He looks up. He wants to say *I love you*, yet like most of his words, they don't surface. Stramit, I think it's called; lots and lots and lots of tiny little pieces of straw pushed together.

She says, I'd like to think that the little pieces stick together because they want to. Y'know — good things fall apart so better things can fall together.

That's so Hollywood, he says.

It's nice to imagine.

You're drunk.

She holds his hand. We're both drunk, Markie.

A neighbour's dog barks, the sound heavy and low through the night.

In the morning, she says, Thanks.

For what?

She shrugs. For being okay. For you.

He squints. Can't really be anyone else.

She appears to say something, or at least attempt to, but then doesn't. And he can't hold her to account for not saying what she wanted to: she's probably seen him do that to her more times than she wants to remember. She leaves just as Georges had, and Markus watches her fade down the track from view.

He sits down on the couch where Elmyra had lain last night. He has a pen, holds it between his index and middle fingers in front of his face. Makes it tilt up and down. He shivers, not because of the cold … just because. Cat's back legs press into his thigh, the place he'd first torn his flesh with Elba's sewing needle. He's taken the bandage off now. The wound's finished its scabbiness. He plays Cold War Kids. He's begun dreaming that

Grayson's real again, and when he wakes, he wants to go back to sleep. A total cliché, y'know, for real. Like: to go back again to peaceful summer evenings, their lethargy, when flies rest and everything holds its breath waiting for nightfall and a temperature drop.

Frost treats pine-wood farm posts with a bluish damp, as it does to the bottoms of trousers. The wattle's (genus *Acacia*) gold sparkles Spartan-like and agrestic, as if he's in another country. Midwinter, the sun is meek, as it's mostly been since April — what, with the lingering clouds and the smoke haze from burnings off. Narioka breathes out a cold fog, left behind by the cold nights, from treetops and swirls it into the space of the Depression. It must creep over the cliffs and into the spare fields of the Plain above. It binds. Unlike the heat of summer, which is restless, this becomes what everyone wishes would go.

It's beginning to fall away. Not the memory — Grayson is falling away. April's gone, May and June. Time becomes impractical, and in each of its moments he understands that another second, minute, hour disappears since the last time he saw *mi compañero*. Even though Grayson is absent, Markus detects him here, physically. And perhaps that's why men believe in gods and goddesses, with their marble-white togas and wreaths of olive in their long flowy hair. Why is it we're told they're very beautiful but they're always out of view? Markus has read some Plato — a gift from Grayson — and he'd got the impression that Ancient Greeks didn't quite believe that Eros existed as a figure; rather, they believed that two people loving one another was Eros embodied, which would go a long way to explaining the exploding in Markus's chest.

Markus's mind is an indissoluble veil of foreign language. Maybe one day it'll make sense. One day. *Mi compañero*. He's not heard that tongue for a while. Out the front window, he watches the evening settle, and ignores twilight's tweak against his skin. The fire's unlit. He puts the pen down to hold his belly. He tries to appease the choppy swell that's threatening to turn his insides into fierce waterspouts, to drown him and make his body bloated and blue.

In the middle of night, a stammered scream bursts up from the middle of his chest. He thrusts his limbs out of his bed and runs to escape down the hallway. He pants, though not from running, rather from the fear of what he's running from. He mistakes his heart for the thump the front door makes when he tosses it open. The sand and stones of the driveway are smooth and cool on the bottoms of his bare feet. He's in his underwear. Sweaty hair sticks to his skin and catches between his eyelids. He subsides. He's been running from a rhythm and now it's caught him up; it's buried itself deep, skirting the boundary of his mind. He's been ignoring its gentle throb. It's pulsing now and he has to let it out. He hears Grayson's voice ascending the dissonance of the pub before he'd been killed.

Mate. It's Rene.

A blanket covers Markus's body. He opens his eyes. They close when the dawn-light enters.

He assumes he sleeps, because the next time he wakes is in the early afternoon. Rene's gone to and from town; groceries packed into green bags sit in the ute's tray. He tells Markus to come help.

Lowering two bags to the ground, his father says, A water main burst in town. The roads were blocked.

Markus takes another two bags and begins walking inside. Rene catches him up. Glass condiment bottles tink together in the bags he's carrying. Markus shrugs and puts the two bags into one hand and opens the laundry door. They're pretending nothing mid-night occurred. They dump the bags on the bench and head back out. Markus looks around at the paddocks.

Yer wanna give us a hand with the garden down front? Rene says.

Markus shrugs. Yair. He isn't morally opposed to work that involves his hands, he's just never thought himself good at it. Ever since he can remember, his father's taught him about the land they live in. Scientific names cascaded from Rene's lips as if ancient spells. *Microlaena stipoides*; *Dacelo novaeguineae*; *Ornithorhynchus anatinus*. One time, early on, Rene told him about hemlock (*Conium maculatum*) — the memory now is sticky-opaque, like the milky poison in the leaves. He only ever absorbed the lines of genus and species and sub-species, but their distinct, overlapping places in the landscape, and how they all fit together — how they all *work* — never quite clicked. He follows his father, like the hopeless apprentice only in for a dollar, to the shed to collect a sapling, then down the drive to the garden at the front.

Rene says, You know that cricketer hit by a ball?

Markus doesn't know more than a whisper he's heard from wherever.

He died. Rene bends over to the soil. Young, too.

Yair.

Y'know the charity footy game?

Markus doesn't speak.

They're gunna give half the money to the family.

What if the family doesn't want it?

Someone else will.

Father and son are on the stretch of land running the length of the drive. Markus imagines that Rene told him to help so as to keep him on an invisible leash, what with last night's antics. Rene also said that Brute said Markus isn't quite right for a mechanic's work.

They're expecting you.

Who?

The coach. The team.

I haven't played a game in years.

They want you to captain, an' it'd make Grayson proud.

Markus scoffs.

Just go to the practice match.

Nah.

I'm not asking you. Rene begins clearing a patch of ground.

Markus shifts the bagged sapling standing between them. The bag's black plastic protects the roots of a red ironbark. They're planting it because it'll provide a good home for bats (various) and boobooks (*Ninox novaeseelandiae*) and, when it's big, some shade for the Murray Greys ... according to his father. Two years full maturity in ideal conditions, his father'd also said. Sky's blue and the sun's harsh, even though it's still winter. Markus has sweat prickle on his back and forehead. Too many clothes. When he woke, it'd been overcast.

Rene says, Fuck, yer'd think it's summer. Drought'll never break in this.

Markus has forgotten about the previous summer's heat. And the drought. The dust, the rabbits, the Burrows' slaughtered livestock and the brittle grass. With the cooler nights of this winter, the idea that the land could be so devoid as to be dead is impossible. Markus says, How do you know?

It's what they say, y'know.

Markus says, It can't be good for the tree, no water and drought.

S'alright, too much'll kill it. Rene takes his eyes out to an unseen place. The blokes over north've gotten rid a trees. Y'know that matchstick tree farm? Work the land too much. He slides his thumb and index finger over a blade of nearby plains grass (*Austrostipa aristiglumis*). An' the soil'll slide right out under 'em. The grass disintegrates as he rolls it between his fingers. Rene stands and shovels a hole, shin-deep to himself and as wide as his own forearm from wrist to elbow. He starts with ease, but each time the blade slices deeper into the soil, Rene grows more tired and more sweaty and more breathless.

A magpie (*Cracticus tibicen*) warbles.

A good tree needs firm roots, healthy soil, nutrition an' water. If the balance is right, bud, the tree'll pay back tenfold. Rene unties the rope binding the black bag around the ironbark's roots, and pulls the plastic away.

The roots are neat, dark in colour, and they lighten as the soil on them air-dries. Smell earthy. There are a number of other, very mature ironbarks lining the driveway with thick-looking bark, gnarled and black, like rot.

When they're done, Rene has to go into town. Order out some business.

Markus, inside the house, sits down in the lounge.

Elba's out selling Herbalife.

There's a huntsman spider (family *Sparassidae*) on the lounge-room floor. Markus keeps it near him by tapping the ground in front of it whenever it turns to scamper away. It's facing him, raising its front legs in the air.

When Markus was younger, he'd sit and watch rainfall

pattering against the glass panes and trickling down. As he grew older, the water wriggling over the window made him think of sex education. The droplets became sperm gametes careening to somewhere out of sight — useless and expired ejaculate. If he were out in the rain, he'd stop and stand and get soaked. Sometimes, he and Grayson came home from school in the rain. After Grayson had left for his own house, Markus'd wait at the driveway. He'd see Grayson's bluish shadow get lighter and lighter the further he went into the grey rain-haze. When Grayson was gone, Markus would watch the water flow down the furrows in the bark of the towering eucalypts in the driveway. Raindrops collected on the leaves of the geraniums below the canopy. The water re-formed at the geranium's leaf tips and dripped onto the greying straw that was spread on the garden beds. He'd rub his face with his palms and then look up at the sky, leaving his mouth open, and squinting because he wanted to be able to see. He'd run up and down the driveway and jump into puddles. His shoes would fill with cold water and his socks, when he took them off later, would smell like wet dog. He did this on the afternoons of rain when Rene wasn't home. He did this then because it was Rene who'd made him, when he was younger, sit in the lounge and watch the rain fall against the glass panes, when all along Markus had wanted to wriggle free.

A tremor against his hand: the huntsman's creeping away. Markus makes a fist and brings it down onto the spider's back. *It'd make Grayson proud.* What on earth could his father have meant by that? Grayson is dead and incapable of pride. It's not even that — it's that Rene had had no interest in Grayson even when Grayson *had* been able to be proud. The pleasurable satisfaction from an act, possession, quality, or relationship by which you measure your stature or self-worth: proud. A relationship … could Rene ever be proud of Markus?

In his room, Markus pulls the sewing needle out. *It'd make Grayson proud.* When the needle pinches and enters his flesh, he doesn't react. And when he begins to bleed, he does not react. He's surprised at how the blood rises out of the wound, like a balloon being inflated by a breath within his thigh. Pleasure derives from this balloon growing and stopping, the glistening bead waiting for the pulsation of his vein. It breaks, or bursts, and spreads over the skin of his thigh as a wet pinkish film, matting the hair near it. He can see a tiny, darker scar left from the first cut he'd made, wriggling on his thigh around the edge and out of sight. He tries to make himself receptive. The needle tears and jabs. His scratches form black calluses on his arm and crystallise like bark. He punches his thigh. It bruises. He drifts.

Rene tells him to get ready for the practice charity football match. A week until the real thing, though the way his father says it sounds like *reel thin*.

Markus prepares himself, i.e. footy gear etc. As he does, a twisting feeling forms in his stomach. He drinks water and vomits it into the toilet. Rene, with Elba in the passenger seat, drives Markus to the oval. While sitting in the backseat of Elba's insurance-Jeep (the one that they gave her after Markus crashed her old one), Markus is thinking that it doesn't matter what you do to try and stop something; it will happen, or won't, depending on heaps-many things not under human control or within human comprehension. Epictetus, which he'd read before Grayson had given him Plato to read. Markus rekindles this Epictetian attitude, words it up to make it sound more profound than the simple *Fuck it* the boys say.

At the footy oval, he finds himself in the toilet. Each of the four cubicles is occupied, and he does not want to piss into the urinal, where the stream will splash onto his shoes as it hits the tray; he'll get stage fright. So, he waits. Each of the four cubicle doors remains open. Men with hands around their fronts train their gazes on their piss. Markus hears the piss spray. His bladder is at the point of being painful. He waits by the wall, pretending to text. The four men finish and are replaced by another four. It's not until this four falls by two that Markus takes up a free cubicle. He locks the cubicle door. Talks himself into trying to piss. His bladder won't release. It seems like ten minutes of pushing before a weak stream starts.

He flushes. The toilets are now empty; the practice game about to start.

Fuck it.

Any other Sunday, he'd've gone with Grayson and got a sausage roll in a roll with tomato sauce, which would ooze out the sides and drop on his palms. Thinking of licking the tangy sauce is better than if he actually ate. He moves his tongue around his empty mouth, pushing it against the places where bubbles of cask wine would fizz, between his teeth, against his lips, on his gums — if it were any other Sunday before. It was better before, because he didn't have to think or reflect. It's all consuming and overwhelming now. You see, before = with. It meant there was no space to fill, because there was walking, and Grayson bringing the cask, and gasping to cool the volcanic mouthful of half-mushed sausage roll.

Markus leaves the room and, in the kitchen, fills the kettle. Boiling water hisses like the kazillion cicadas on hot nights when Grayson and he had gone camping. They'd set out with a two-man tent and fishing rods. That was year eight or nine. They stayed wide-eyed to the break of dawn.

Markus hears a *thunk* and then another. He sees through the kitchen window, standing outside Rene's shed, Buff Burrows.

Buff has a yet untouched slab of round wood, a rope tied over its middle, at his feet. He's wearing a long-sleeved red-checked flannel shirt, its front buttons undone, even in this cold, to reveal a tight-white singlet underneath. He's wearing his footy shorts from yesterday's practice match and has changed his footy boots for Blundstones. Buff raises the maul, its blade glinting.

Markus heads out there. He drags his feet a few times in the sandy yard and sits down on a spare chopping block. Nearby is a small pile of wood Buff's already cut.

Markus says, Who sent you around?

Thunk: the maul's blade hits the centre of the wood. A crack appears.

Buff says, What happened there? He nods to where Markus's motorbike used to stand. Buff's biceps kind of tense when the maul's above his head and then ripple when the blade cuts into the timber. Rigid, controlled momentum paired with strength.

Still fucked, Markus says.

Thunk: hits the log at a small angle from the first cut to make a wedge of wood.

Fucken unreliable.

Markus plays with his leg hair. What are you doing here?

I told y'at footy.

Markus doesn't recall.

Said I'd come t' help you an' Ren out.

Thunk: working clockwise around the log, cutting cake wedges. The rope around the middle keeps each wedge placed even as he slices the log itself apart.

Markus moves to the prep table pushed up against the wall inside Rene's shed. On the table, small plastic pots: rows of geranium and eucalyptus. Of the latter, he'd felled a fully-grown specimen back in the summer, the same wood Buff's now slicing. Markus picks one of the seedlings up. Its leaves move in similar rhythms to a butterfly's wings.

Buff asks if he's heard from Cecily. He's surely after something — why else would he be here of his own accord? To chop wood? Bullshit.

Bellos, Buff huffs.

Markus replaces the pot. He hoicks onto the shed's floor.

You're a shit bloke, Buff says, puffy and husky, his words like dirty coal from a mine.

Markus watches Buff pull the maul's blade from the wood. Elmyra was here the other day, he says.

She told me.

No Marilyn.

Would it've been different if she was? Buff's a mostly harmless mosquito, silently landing and putting his own saliva, laced with anti-coagulant, into your veins before drawing back your blood. Give and take. Blond hair and marble skin as threateningly incendiary as the sun. Elmyra's intoxicated with him.

Probably not, says Markus, but quiet enough that only he can hear.

At some point, Markus, too, had almost succumbed to the same heady, deadened masculinity Buff Burrows spreads about him. When Buff first appeared in the area, armoured in dark Ray-Bans and unflattering beige cargo shorts. At football training. Buff had said he's a wingman. Markus, as then-captain, said, We'll put you in mid-field. Wings are useless. Fully prepared to go the distance, Markus had made him vice-captain. And, in line with his responsibilities, Buff spoke out at anyone who spoke out at Markus.

But none of that really matters now — not footy, not Buff, not captains and vices, not speaking out or staying silent.

Markus worries that the pressure he feels inside himself — if released — will rip through his entire body like a white-head pustule on his late-pubescent face. He says, Leave you to it then. And as he walks away from Buff, he tells himself he's prevented someone else from having to clean his blood-pus mess off the mirror.

Patchy sky of grey clouds. Some holes where the blue sky can be seen: a broken mosaic. Or a whole mosaic? Whatever. Sunbeams don't shine on him or near the ground around him; rather, the beams make landfall beyond his sight, on distant countryside. Other mornings, the sun's rays hit a paddock a few hundred metres away. And on these mornings, it's as if he and the room he stands in are a far too shadowed place within his subconscious. Forever out of his way. Like Byron's *estrella de la mañana de la memoria*. Spanish sticks, as does the recollection of the accent Grayson would do to keep them going through the double periods before lunch. For a week or so now, Markus has been trying to dissect the language, which at school he never had, but which Grayson spoke so finely. Is it *de la recuerdo* instead?

¿Puedo ir al baño? Grayson would rub his jumper where his bladder might've been. He pointed at the door.

Sólo si realmente eres, Teacher replied.

Grayson laughed and then said, *Donde voy no es nada para usted preocuparse.*

Teacher smiled, *Hazlo rápido, niño descarado.*

And Grayson leant to Markus and whispered, *Me estoy saliendo, amigo. Tu elección si quieres venir.*

How can it be that Markus is heading forward and at the same time going back? Disassociating from the present, i.e., not in the so-called *now*, as he used to be. He's associated in the reality of memory and imagination.

A week. A week. His room is lived in, smells lived-in, too. He opens the curtains. On the floor, sunlight falls. He thinks of Moses and the Israelites. Purple linen, censers and scents, glints of tabernacle gold — *alpha chi rho omega* make the phrase *I Rule*. What does discovering any of that mean to him?

Rene calls him. Over the phone, he tells Markus to be ready when he gets home because today is the actual charity football match.

Back at the bedroom window, Markus sees it has light streaks across it because of the angle the sun's coming at it. The pane shakes from the wind. The bright, slim streaks, three or four of them, slant in front of his face. He peers between two of the lines to the yard beyond. He raises his fist, pushes it toward the glass. Stops. He tips his fist and taps on the glass with his knuckles. Pulls away and thrusts his fist back again. Stops. Lowers his fist and rests his forehead on the window.

Rene's ute comes up the driveway.

Markus switches the bathroom's radio on and is greeted by Lewis McKirdy's voice. He waits for the music. Lewis is going on, getting annoying. Fuck. Markus switches the radio off and puts his iPod into the dock. When he's dried and re-underweared, he watches himself in the mirror as he slides his razor over his neck, past his Adam's apple. When he's done he washes the excess shaving foam away, and, with drips off his chin and dribbles on his cheek, Markus pummels his reflection with both his fists. He dresses in trackies, a blue shirt, and a white hoodie with a print of LSP saying, 'What the lump?' Footy stuff and other shit together, he heads to the open-plan area.

I'm not magnificent. I'm not magnificent, special, happy, or light. I'm dark. Sunken. An unseen iceberg in the Southern Ocean: grey-white, bobbing and spumeless. I'll melt away because of rising sea temperatures and become water, rain, and salt to taint freshwater supplies. I'll be the drought.

Markus's breath forms a grey patch on the ute's window as the vehicle turns into the footy ground.

Rene drops him out back of the change rooms.

The shower room is a large sandstone cube that acts as a small divider, built in the middle of the change room's tin outer. The shower block has two entries: one for the home team and one for the away team (home: those living in Narioka; away: those from the farmlands). These entries oppose each other, and through each is the respective change room. Markus used to tell everyone the sandstone was asbestos, and he'd throw little chunks that had fallen from the edges at his teammates, at their feet as they showered, in their hair as they dressed, into their bags. Today, he prefers the soft crunching of the fallen-away chunks as he steps on them.

His duffel bag slaps on the polished concrete floor.

Buff stands beside him, naked from a pre-game shower. His pink junk. His firm muscles. He's mostly firm. And yet, where there are fine blond hairs coating his thighs and arse, these limbs, especially his arse, quiver each time he steps around. He's starting to dress: pulling up jocks, the black and red footy shorts over the top, a Guernsey. The quiver in his looser areas is slight, and makes the built-up areas seem to be hiding his *self* beneath, as if his self begs on hands and knees to be noticed at all.

Markus shrugs. He pulls on the red-and-black Guernsey, like Essendon, he'd once thought. It puffs against his skin. Whiffs of athletic rub come in draughts: hot-cutting and comforting before play. The grassy oval will be dew and frost. The wind driving down centre field will be shards of ice. Coldness makes cracking his fingers painful. He disbelieves that cracking knuckles causes arthritis. Keeping the joints uncracked hurts more. He takes each finger, bent over, and presses it down into itself. It may crack. It may not. Sitting on the low wood bench along the dim change room's wall, he does this to his fingers. One doesn't get the pain and the release. He stretches out the uncracked finger, an index finger, to see if it needs warming up, then presses it down again. It doesn't crack. He pushes harder. The knuckle turns white and the creases go deep red, like they're going to split his skin open.

Ya gunna break it off, Coach yells.

Markus rests his hands between his legs.

Buff says, Fucken spastic.

The coach gives a pre-game speech: grit, determination, teamwork. An' piss orf if yer not up fer it! The team, two by two, leaves the shed and heads out onto the foggy field. The silence has a sound: hushed static, as if tuning in for signs of life. The fog means most can't see the scratches running tracks up Markus's arms or the callouses from the sewing needle criss-crossing his thighs. No doubt, someone caught sight of them back in the change room. None said a word. The skimpy footy outfit tells the story; walking in the fog is like walking through cottonwool. Filling up his ribcage: the siren. Young men's reckless bodies thud to the earth and the ump's whistle is shrill. Markus can't see where the bodies collide or where words from restless mouths shout at him to run left. Left he goes. Through a stretching hole in the fog a red Sherrin pirouettes and drops into his hands. *Thoof.* He spins, boots it out of sight. Cheers. Car horns. Noise rises up into his ears. Snap of the goalkeeper's flags. A whistle. He focuses on his thumping heart. It's aural, internal. Echoing. He punches himself in the gut, and its contents spill out, yellow frothy bile, onto the field.

You right? It's the Youarang kid come running over. His hand's on Markus's back.

Markus nods, stands up and says, Yair. He wipes the corner of his mouth with the back of his hand.

Youarang sniffs a laugh and says, Nah, mate. He whacks Markus gently on the shoulder. Why don't you head back to the rooms — foggy as all get out here, Coach won't even notice one less. Youarang whacks him once more. Go.

Markus crumples onto the yellowish tiles inside the shower block. His shins are bruised and his silky shorts stained by grass and mud. His hair drips murky water. There's no one else here. Hot water from the showerhead above hisses and slaps against Markus and the tiles he's sitting on. The noises outside are deadened by the chamber of sandstone. He disregards those things he cannot see. Almost, for there's always one thing he can't escape. This thing has been split up as many things. Now, the splits forge, and the gap between the things he can't see and can't touch closes and joins into the singular thing they've always been. Just now, in this shower block, they come into involuntary, premature realisation. Knees drawn to his chest, arms hugging his legs, head hung in the hissing water — he can feel himself as if he's beating with clenched fists on Grayson's grave.

You in here, Bellos? The tacks on the bottoms of Buff's boots crunch over the concrete, making it sound like a thick layer of gravel. The athletic rub scent wavers in the air. Buff leans against the door's jamb and says, You'rang said y'chucked on field.

Markus looks at the tiles near his toes and says, It was behind play.

Buff starts to untie his boots. Why?

Because.

'Cause why?

Because.

You sick? Buff takes his first boot off.

Markus doesn't reply.

Buff begins wrestling the second sodden boot. His arm's skin is white, exposed and even; with his bulging biceps and square-set shoulders, he is buried inside the Guernsey. Or perhaps it's burying itself into him, an entire sporting code seeping from the dyed cotton through his white skin and into his healthy veins. Buff Burrows. He is … what? Small. He's taking the other boot off, throwing it behind him into the change room. He's playing with the fluff on the tips of his footy socks. His shorts are too short, and from the way he's sitting, Markus can see his yellow underwear and the outline of his junk.

Another update on the railway appears in the *Leader*: a tradie injures himself while attending the construction site. He, along with his colleagues, had resumed work when he slipped on loose earth and broke his arm. Inquiries, investigations, paperwork will hold up construction.

Markus is standing beside the kitchen table. Through the glass door, he sees his father in one of the veggie patches out back. Rene has a tiny paintbrush in one hand, which he's using to transfer pollen from one flower to the stamen of a flower of the same species. The bees who used to pollinate the crops all over Narioka stopped arriving a year or so back. Markus closes the newspaper. Takes his coffee in his hands. He closes his eyes.

Try again.

There's a smudgeable layer of oil or grease on the table top. He rubs hard. It relocates itself on the pad of his finger. He makes another cuppa. Tea this time, and the bag's left in, and the water goes this crazy peachy colour that reminds him of the sunrise. Cold War Kids plays from the dock sitting underneath the telly. He can't name the tune. There's afternoon coming in, shining across the iPod's screen and blocking the song's title. Saying it aloud, a whisper will do. Y'know. The tongue's rebellious, and the words it flicks are futile and never come out to mean what is intended. What could I say? He bangs his fist into his thigh, alternating hard and soft. He can never speak aloud what's inside. A paralysis.

Markus winces.

He loves Grayson.

Tea spills down the side of the cup.

Markus hates that he loves Grayson, because he tells himself he hates men. He finds people repulsive. People and their relationships. Especially men. Repulsive. Rene: drove his first wife away with a glass of gin and a well-aimed fist. Buff: billowing with maleness he hasn't a hold on. Georges: dirty sanchez.

Men are repulsive. With their sex. With their hair. Their physicality. With their laughs and deep voices and motives and desires and kisses and hands, searching-seeking hands searching and seeking minds and fingers and tongues and lips and beards and stubble. Men. Cocks and balls and fucks and butts and ribs and thighs and ears. Their eyes, deep blue or the-always-loveliest brown eyes, and wrinkled faces when the sun's shining in their brown eyes. Like earth. Like death. Regeneration. Life. Growth. Nutrition. Men with their thoughts. Men with their minds again and again. Their hearts and wanting to fill their hearts with love. Selfish love. Fuck their love. He shouldn't have a life he never asked for and be expected to love men. With their problems never spoken outward. And childhood trauma and family issues. Men wanting to be held or hold. Markus laughs or sniffs or huffs. Perhaps growls.

To let someone love him: they say you shouldn't use the word 'love' — you should show it. Yet when the person he loves lies six feet beneath the surface, there's little *except* the abstract nature of words to describe, or not, what he feels inside.

Outside him, out there in the small microcosm his father's creating, the veggies Rene hand-pollinated fatten in the warming months, engorging themselves with sunlight and becoming rosy in the cheeks. Around them the cicadas sing, above them cockatoos screak, and between the full pumpkins and bundles of cherry tomatoes the cabbage butterflies flick and whisk. Inside, away from all this, Markus's nineteenth birthday passes. Onward and upward. The charity footy match is never spoken of again, the money raised never quoted. Buff reports that his dad said it was a huge success. A thank-you note in the mail and all. And Elmyra's doing whatever she's doing, her Marilyn unseen since before Grayson died. Markus begins work for his father, because Brute said he wasn't fit for the apprenticeship. So, Markus works on the farm's books, the paperwork, the finances, that drib-drab correspondence with the bank manager. Rene's in a bit of money trouble. Markus doesn't say; instead, he tries to find the money where he can and sweet-talk the bank some more.

Elba says, You're talking more quietly than usual.

He says, I'm not — you're not listening at your usual.

She laughs.

He turns the muscles in his face into the shape of an orange quarter.

She asks him, How're you doing?

And he says, Fine.

And she says, How are you, really?

And he says, Really, I'm fine.

And she goes to speak again, stops. With tight lips she smiles once more. She mostly leaves him be, continuing to sell Herbalife in town five days a week. Leaving Markus each day to begin the farm's books, leaving him to wait for the mail. He peeks through the lace at every car that passes. The tyres hush over the crumbling bitumen at the end of the driveway. He makes sure his mind doesn't forget about the stars, the night, the long-gone rain and wind and the cold, the shivering on the ground and the headlights flickering on, off, on, off, and the nothing, the calling out, the out calling, the crying out and the crying and the rain. The unfound. One morning, he gives up waiting earlier than usual. He turns from the window and drinks his coffee. None left. Makes a fourth and sits at the table, his back to the lounge and its window and to the mailbox, turned away from the road and remembrances. He drinks the coffee and in between sips, he bites his top lip. Peels its skin away. With each coffee sip and each intermittent bite, his lip becomes more sensitive. The steaming liquid burns his exposed lip and makes it bleed. When he pulls back the cup, he sees a tiny swirl of blood in the liquid. Tie-dye. Behind him, he hears a car slow down. The mailperson.

The *Leader* says they've restarted rail work, begun installing the actual railway. Markus looks at the images in the wrap-around special. Flat, long, and endless, a foundation of ballasts and sleepers ready to have rails laid. A few sleepers have been stolen and others turned over or misplaced.

Buff says that he wants to come around and tinker with Rene's muscle car. Markus didn't know that Rene had a muscle car. While he waits for Buff, Markus stands near the shed. He eats a banana and watches mud-dauber wasps (*Sceliphron sp.*) skirt across the dirt. Supposes they mustn't do pollination, then.

Buff's car speeds up the drive, trailing dust. He brakes and slams the door shut as he exits.

Cicadas fill the pause.

Ya didn't show up at footy pre-season.

Markus says, I had work.

Coach asked for ya.

Yair.

Right. Look, I shoulda bin around after ya.

Markus says, It's alright, and the convo dies.

The muscle car is kept under a black sheet; beneath, its duco is east sky at twilight. The chassis hugs the shed's floor, looking clever.

Straight from the showroom, Buff says. He hovers his fingers over the bonnet. Imagine how fast it'd go.

Tracey Chapman comes to mind. Markus looks around for his father. Guess the shed's too dark, I didn't see it, he says.

Or Ren didn't want you to know about it. Buff's done a full circle around the vehicle, checked every window and even smelled it. Dad an' I are goin' pig huntin', he finally says.

Markus nods.

You should come.

Markus shakes his head.

Dad didn't give a choice, Buff says, replacing the sheet over the car. Said y'need t' get off this property.

I work here.

He said y'shouldn't work where ya live.

What else am I supposed to do here? Markus gestures with his hand to the purlieus, the paddocks that he cannot see through the shed's walls of tin.

Buff shrugs.

I always do shit for people, Markus says.

Dad's just lookin' out for ya. Buff's weighing the sheet down on the ground with bricks, readjusting it not-too-tight, so as not to damage the car.

The next day, before the Burrows are to pick up Markus for the pig-hunting trip, a letter with legal insignia arrives addressed to a Mr M. W. Bello. A court summons for a hearing in some months' time.

Rene says, She'll be right — yer haven't driven for a year, got no priors, yer young. And remorseful, yair?

Markus sits in the back seat of Brute's car. Buff's driving. They head to the bush around the Lake. Buff rests two shotguns against a sapling. By mid-arvo, they're hunting.

It's not the killing of the pig that creeps Markus out the most; he supports removal of pests from where they don't belong. Rene taught him that. Someone, maybe Cecily, once said that humans should be removed then, too: we don't belong here. The feral pig is smaller and leaner and more muscular than a domestic pig. It's got sinewy shoulders and neck, which remind him of an animal far grander — i.e. a wildebeest, though this pig, this mangy thing, is more thin and coarse. It has a long snout and tusks. Its tail is straight, with a bushy tip. Markus had been expecting a curly tail. It's disturbing, never mind the coughing gurgle it's making as the leftover air escapes its lungs. The blood: fine, bright, syrupy blood creeping through the boar's hair. It makes him shiver.

Brute calls Markus a pussy.

Buff bends down beside his father, who's wrestling the pig's head into a position. Blood oozes out the pig's left nostril. The Burrows look up from under their wide-brimmed hats. The sun brightens the scene, makes them squint, and Buff tilts his head toward his father.

Markus lines them up in the phone's screen, because they've asked him to take a photo. It's unbalanced. Too much weight. Too much emphasis on the people and not the pig — not enough emphasis on the pig's wounds, which their friends in Narioka will admire when they look at this picture on Facebook. Markus moves toward the pig, grabs its ear. Warm. Perhaps not quite dead. Warm, and disgusting for being warm. It's meant to be dead. Should be cold and vacant. Yet the glint of its eye hasn't vacated. Markus pushes the limp pig's head toward Brute and Buff, and the shotgun wound settles between them to show off torn ligament and shattered flesh. Brute was close when he was demonstrating to Buff how to shoot proper-point-blank in the neck. After readjusting the carcass, Markus steps back and realigns the men and the pig in the frame of Buff's smartphone.

Back at the campsite, Brute drags the boar from the ute's tray and then some distance away from their camp. Buff takes off his hat. He fills a plastic tub with water and rubs his hands in the liquid. Dirt and blood from the boar wash away. When he's done, he walks to a nearby ironbark and pours the pink-tinted water at its base. Markus sits in a camp chair beside the fire, somewhat aware of Buff's father hacking into the dirty flesh of a gigantic pig. He draws a random pattern in the dirt with the end of a stick he's holding.

Buff sits beside him. Says, What d'you think?

About?

The hunt, he chuckles.

Markus shrugs.

Yer reckon it felt much?

What?

The pig.

Maybe at the start.

Yair. Buff's picking stuff out from under his fingernails.

Markus says, It's for the best. He's thinking of the time this very situation had been reversed, when Buff had dropped a live mouse into Snake's tank to be killed. He's thinking how one event can flip over on its head.

Buff nods. Course, didn't say otherwise, did I.

Nah, says Markus. He tosses the stick into the fire.

When the Burrows first moved into the region — father, mother, son — they bought the most expensive farm out the other side of Narioka. Prime real estate.

The Burrows family enjoyed aloneness in this arrangement, away from the goings-on of Narioka, eating dinner each night illuminated by the TV screen. Brute brought with him a mythology of rebellion — a bikie from a city club or some shit — though Markus never bought into it. At the first footy training Brute attended, Markus watched him drop a punt and then grab his hamstring as the ball fell wide of the goalposts. Despite this inaccuracy, the Burrows, from what Markus has seen over the years, are outward, upfront, and would rather chip-in to the community before they chipped in for each other. Buff's mother is the chair of the PTA and president at the local netball club — always in the pub with a raffle board for one or the other. Brute, as the local mechanic, kept the town in motion and, in turn, the town kept him as both ruck rover and captain of the first eighteen. Their son, Buff, left to his own devices, pinged back and forth across the Depression. He vaunted his muscles, such as at the school swimming carnivals and even athletics day, though he insisted he went shirtless because of tags. In those sunglasses, shielding his eyes from the world, he spat out his hatred of any tag that scratched his neck: size tags, brand tags, name tags. He'd kick a shirt he tossed on the ground and complain, Companies fucken stitch tags into material so I can't cut 'em away.

After the hunting trip, Rene's asked him to put out a load of washing. Markus, the kitchen's cool slate tile underfoot, instead fills a glass with boiling water and bi-carb soda and into it drops his top and bottom retainers. The bubbles fizz about the blue plastic moulds. With the glass in hand, he goes to the lounge and switches the AC on. He goes to his room, sits the glass on his bedside table. He falls onto his bed and covers himself with the doona. Throws it back because it's far too hot for that. The heat irritates and makes him want to flick the taut skin covering his stomach.

Elba will be home soon. Maybe she'll be hungry. He should cook. *Pfft.* He's not her mother nor is she his mother. And she's damn well not *Elba.* She's Samantha, and everyone in town knows that Samantha became Elba. *¡Hola! Me llamo. Me nombré es Elba. May YAH-moh. Soy Elba.* She'd taken a retreat trip to Spain three or four years back, which she maintains was paid for and run by Herbalife. Gone a week, two, maybe three. Upon her impending return, she'd phoned ahead. Gather in the lounge, she informed Rene over the phone. I've some news. Perhaps she'd said it in Spanish. On the day when Samantha was to arrive, Markus'd grabbed Cat and sat beside Rene on the couch. They hadn't yet got an AC, so they were sticky-hot. Markus'd been in his undies prior to Samantha's arrival, at least until his father thundered, Y'ain't a Hilfiger model, now get in ya fucken clothes. Rene flicked over the pages of the *Leader* until he heard a car horn toot twice and jolted to his feet. Cat crouched low at this, eyes wide, ears back, claws dug deeper into Markus's bare skin: needles piercing his thigh. Samantha came in, wearing a flowy orange flamenco-type skirt and a white sleeveless calico shirt, along with clunky jewellery. The top two buttons of her shirt were undone. Her hair was loose, wavy, darker, and it somehow made her green eyes illuminate.

From that day to this, and into the coming days, she is called Elba. Sometimes he wants to tear the clothes, tear the Spanish, from Elba. She's more than that. She's like Elmyra — both trying to forge identities in the confines of this small town. That's what makes the men in the pub point them out. But he can't tear their clothes away, because perhaps they'd tear his away in return … He hears the sound of a car in the distance. He shifts to the end of the mattress and reaches to close his bedroom door. It slams. He presses play on his music dock and the sound comes loud enough to signal *don't disturb*. He tosses around a bit. The mattress holds the warmth from his body and intensifies it. He flops onto the floor. Even the floor, raised as it is off the ground by stilts, cannot escape the heat coming inside and making itself comfortable. The carpet bites into his back. A gap in the curtains releases a shaft of sunlight diagonally over his chest. Sweat pricking on his forehead.

The last two editions of the *Leader* have said that there might not be enough water to fill the public swimming pool this summer. The picture accompanying the articles both times was the Mayor and the lifeguard, that Youarang kid. The picture showed the Mayor standing on the pavement outside the pool's cyclone-wire fence and Youarang inside the fence. Golden grass abounded. Youarang insisted that they make the pool full for summer to keep wayward youth off the street. The Mayor says, We're here to do what's best for the community, and if that means withholding water from the public pool for water on the farms, so be it.

Markus heads into the lounge, where Elba's laying on the couch in the cool and dark; one forearm rests against her forehead, the other hand on her belly.

He announces that he's going for a swim.

She lifts her head to say, Don't drown.

He pokes his tongue out at her and exits through the front. He makes his way into town, doesn't pay attention to which way he's going. This place is familiar and his feet know their way. Besides, the pool is his focus, not how he gets there. The sudden need for water, for cool-blue, is possessing.

When he arrives, the pool is waterless. Was he expecting a fairy-tale ending? What, because he's had a hard time? Yair. Right. Through the cyclone fence, Markus sees a dark crusty line against the side of the pool from where the water used to rest. On the front gate is a paper sign. *There'll be no swimming this summer.* He pulls the pen out from his pocket and writes beneath *you can if you like, mind your head on the bottom.* When he turns away, his vision is obstructed: the bright sunlight reflecting off the white-paper note burnt into his pupils. A few moments, his eyes have readjusted. Clear. Turning away from the locked gates, he is paying attention to the scratchings in the pavement and the trodden-down chewing gum when he bumps into another person out here on the quiet street.

It's Cecily. Her skin paler than the last time he saw her — which was in her togs, sitting beside Grayson at the pool. Her lips thinner than when they had maneuvered cherry-flavoured ice cream into her mouth; today, they're ajar as if she's breathless. She puts her hand on her stomach.

Without any witnesses, he speaks to her directly: What are you doing here?

I live here. She hitches her duffle bag up on her shoulder. And I could ask you the same. She's not looking at him; she's wearing sunglasses, though, so could be casting side glances.

I came to see if the newspaper article about the pool was true, he says.

She nods. Same.

He wants her to hold him responsible, to smash his face into the contorted cyclone wire. He peers at her, pleading her to place it all on him. To make it known he's solely responsible.

Yet she says, I tried to call you heaps of times.

I know.

To no answer.

I know.

All I wanted was to … I dunno, she says and shrugs at the same time.

He finally looks away, across to the empty creek. He's certain this is the end. He says, We could get a coffee? The words as bitter in his mouth as the burnt coffee he's just suggested they should get.

She scoffs, spilling a scolding of embarrassment over his skin. It's too late for that, she says. She hitches up her duffel bag once more and goes to step around him.

He touches her elbow and says, I love him.

She might have blinked, long and slow, before she answers. So do I. She removes herself from his touch and heads down the empty street, searching for a different pool to swim in.

Feeling defeated, and without any water to hold him afloat, his days are disposed of by doing very little. Blue seeps into his mind, perhaps because of the heat, the absence of water. Blue light in stained-glass. He catches sight of it out the corner of his eye. Reflective blue, sky-high soaring blue, deep blue. Blue eyes. He can never focus on it, but he can't escape it either. Recently, it's been getting closer to ceremonious blue, the colour of regret.

Or the violet-blue shade of the official flower of Derby Day at far-off Flemington — cornflower (*Centaurea cyanus*): that flower, on purpose, conflicts with the upcoming yellow-gold rose of Tuesday's grander Cup. Rene's betting two bucks each way on each race; he sips mineral waters on ice, with a slice of lemon. Elba's done a platter of tonally different cheeses, cured meats and fruit, and one or two dips of questionable colour. Markus drops a grand on the nose of the clear favourite, but he loses it all when some 100–1 shot cuts through the pack to claim the win.

Despite the work he's doing for the farm's books, right through to Christmas Rene is at him. Ya need a proper job. Markus is surprised his father doesn't count the bookwork and money-finding as proper work. The north winds get drier, hotter, stronger. Good washing days, Markus says to Elba. She looks at him, smiles and says, Well, we best get to it.

On Boxing Day, Rene makes him play backyard cricket. The kerbside bin's the stumps. Rene bowls from near the house. Six and out, no LBs, auto wikie. The radio's crackling. The Test at the 'G is almost understandable. Elba sits under the shade of a few stray oleanders, which Rene's yet to remove and poison.

At the end of the week, Rene and Elba go into town on New Year's Eve. No fireworks: total fire ban. Markus says he'll stay home. No point without fireworks. He watches *Round The Twist* and drinks beer.

And in time, Markus's twentieth birthday passes in the form of a chocolate mud-cake from the IGA and home-brand fizzy drink. Rene's working hard, and comes in from the land at nine or ten pm to say, Thistles've blown in from the next property over — 'bout a k 'way. Took longer than expected to chip them out.

By mid-February, Rene's at it again. Ya need a proper job.

Where in this desolation? Markus, instead, keeps to his father's farm's books. The money trouble doesn't worsen or improve.

And then autumn's mid-way through its moods. Outside, none of the leaves drop: the trees keep hold of them as if pulling a woolly jumper tighter around their branches. The grass begins to green. A fake green that'll turn yellow with the faintest lick of heat.

Winter's darkness rises at six in the evening. Days shorten. When not filled with cloud or fog, the sky's heavy. He wants it to fall to the earth and fill the Depression to the brim.

Markus looks at the weave in the carpet. The fibres bind themselves up with one another. He attempts to unpick them: Platonic union will always end in undoing. An hour later, he's showered and dressed. It's not much. It's enough. Black and grey, as if for a funeral. The suit's tight over his chest and pinches a little under his arms.

Rene says, Shirt looks better tucked in.

It's otherworldly. A court appearance is otherworldly. A world of murder in dank alleys and drug busts in ghettos. Somehow, Markus has fallen to the other side of the tracks. You don't have to deal with that side unless you do something otherworldly. He gets a waft of new-leather from his shoes. Their stiff heels bite into his ankle's soft flesh. The mirror shows him his own blank eyes, which say he's not ready.

Narioka's courthouse is a solid red-brick structure. It holds a single courtroom surrounded on three sides by offices. The façade is elaborate, flanked by timber and a cast-iron bullnose veranda. The ridged slate roof is decorated with railings and finials. The gable reaches an interesting culmination, though none can actually see the culmination because it reaches too high for prying eyes — passers-by just assume it's interesting. When judges are not using the rooms — which they do just once a month — local growers use them to sell produce from. The judge, in gown and cap, sits behind a wooden desk, which is too elaborate for this rurality. The judge is small, and appears lost in the elongated grain and tight knots and growth rings and burls and slubs. Most of the room's interior is composed of wood: it is as if Markus has been transported inside the trunk of a giant eucalypt, like a bardi grub under instruction from the barrister he has met today. He, or rather the pro bono barrister, pleads guilty to one count of dangerous driving. Evidence is presented, questions asked, points contested, flipped, proven, shushed-up. Markus watches, through the windows, the blue sky outside and some cockatoos flapping past.

No rain falls. They say the drought's broken in the city — a pipeline is *their* saviour. Yet, it's hard to keep the city's reservoirs full when they're thirty-two per cent, slowly falling, and there's no water left here in the Depression for them to pipe away.

In bed, Markus rolls over to his stomach. The new position draws out stiffness in his lower back. Waking in the same room that he fell asleep in isn't enough. As he clamps shut his eyes, he wishes he'd remained asleep.

A day after his sentencing, Markus is the same.

He'd gotten home the previous night and cried in the bottom of the shower. No release, just salty water running in with the clean and washing away down the drain. He'd used Elba's sewing needle to cut open his skin. No release, just stinging in the shower and even that, the pain, no longer calmed him. What he assumes the judicial system intends as a release — the sentence — is rather anticlimactic. As far as the judge is concerned, the case is finished, and in a fortnight, Markus will begin community service as a council worker, weeding at the side of the road, marking lines in the middle of it, mowing the lawn beside the public swimming pool. Wearing a high-visibility vest won't make the deceased visible.

It was the farmer first on scene who'd stuck more than anything else.

The farmer had asked, You okay?

Markus nodded. Just a little tired, he said.

Stay awake and count for me.

One two three four …

You the only one in the car? the farmer asked.

No, Markus said.

Was there two of ya, son? More?

Markus nodded. Two. But I don't know where he is now.

Help'll be here soon, the farmer said.

Can you help me find him?

I don't think we will.

How can you know that?

The farmer patted Markus's shoulder. Are ya right? the farmer asked.

Markus nodded. It could be worse.

You're alive, aren't ya.

Yair.

Son, the farmer said, ya need to sit down for a minute.

But what about my friend?

Sit on the grass, the farmer said. The ambos are here.

Can you get my friend?

The ambos want to look ya over.

Where's Grayson?

C'mon, son, the farmer said.

You know where Grayson is, don't you?

The farmer nodded.

Please tell me?

Afterward, the local sergeant said, We'll be in contact soon.

Rene drove Markus home from the scene, and neither of them said a word. It was a long while ago if counting the days chronologically and rather inadequate if measuring by your own peculiar sense of time. They'd pulled up out back of Rene's as the sun began to raise its golden head: a sleepy teenager yawning through fairy-floss pink clouds and breaking the robin-egg blue. Last night's violent storm was nothing more than the four smashed hanging pots lying on the veranda's brickwork. Markus looked at the mud on his hands, under his nails, the redder stuff up his arms; he looked at his torn jeans and punctured shirt. Inside the house, he'd stripped to his undies and slipped beneath the cold doona. Tears came. Kept coming and he gasped. When he could no longer hear the sounds of Rene or Elba, he took his swimming bag and left the house. The distinct claustrophobia of safety was too much. He walked out into a high sun. He walked the back roads. He walked to the public pool (which had still had water in it). It was empty of people.

Didn't reckon we'd be seeing you this morning, said Youarang, who stood in the dim entry room with the ice-creams and packet chips and Python snakes, wearing his glary yellow YMCA lifesaver t-shirt.

Markus went there to feel exhausted, to feel his body burn and burst, just like most other mornings; however, this morning, he contemplated letting the water extinguish him.

Standing in the mid-section of the public pool, the water was ice-blue cool on Markus's skin. A car hushed past on Melville Street. Gone before he saw it. He looked at the replica steam-train in the rose gardens beside the empty creek before he sank beneath the water. He let his back touch the bottom. He couldn't decide where the surface ended and the sky began. He screamed into the water. What he screamed was an attempt to push the crushing weight suffocating his chest out of him. The air bubbles from his lungs rattled the water, rushing to the surface as if his scream had boiled it. When there was no air left in him, he considered breathing in. Instead, he put his feet on the semi-slimy bottom and followed his bubbles upward, onward. He swashed the mud and dried blood from his body until he was clean. Picking out the same stuff stuck under his fingernails took the longest. He swam next. Lap after lap of breaststroke, kicking against the water, splitting it and dragging it behind him with his palms. Lap after lap, until he was dry-retching above the overflow drain that runs around the rim of the pool.

At home, he'd made his way to the bathroom. Put the radio on. He'd looked at himself in the mirror for a long time and had clenched at the pain in his shoulder — he could remember that side of his body hitting the driver's door when the car flipped. He hoped it'd bruise. He let go of the shoulder. Clenched again.

He found the traces that Grayson had left behind after he had stayed over two nights ago, after Markus's eighteenth birthday. There was an un-hung towel and the Vegemite jar out on the bench, with further evidence of its use — a dirty knife and plate — in the sink. These traces annoyed Markus as he followed them around the house, because he was the one who had to clean them up and it was like Grayson was dying again. But touching them, picking them up — running his fingers over the dried-out towel — he realised that these things were some of the last things Grayson had touched. And this made Markus appreciate them. These traces of Grayson were a strange currency that Markus felt comfortable using in the days following Grayson's death. An economy he used to buy the next day, and the next. Even after the towel had been hung out on the line, smelling of rosy fabric softener. Even after the plate and knife were put away, sparkling.

Elba was on the couch, her auburn hair black in the dim room, her dress lying against her skin as if it were a blanket. Her damp hair hung off her forehead. The plastic blinds drawn over the lounge room's windows clacked against the sill. Markus imagined blowing Elba's dress away, as he would a tissue from the bench into the bin. She snored. The telly was playing a repeat of *Seinfeld*. He decided it wasn't funny, turned it over to *The Amazing World Of Gumball*. It wasn't any funnier, but it made him forget the world for the show's duration.

He woke when it was dark.

Rene'd replaced Elba on the couch, and the telly had *Seinfeld* back. Rene told him, We're gunna have a bonfire out back.

Markus said, I'll be right.

Rene said, It's for you.

And Markus had agreed. Too tired to argue or, rather, too light — there it was again: light. He said, I can't stay up too late, my apprenticeship starts tomorrow.

Nah, bud. It's sorted. I spoke with Brute. Says start when y'ready.

While Markus waited for the fire, he deleted all the apps from his phone. Facebook, Snapchat, Insta, Words with Friends. He took the battery and SIM out. Tried to stop anyone from getting in his head. He placed his mobile in the same snap-lock plastic bag Elba had presented a rock from Uluru to him in only a few days ago. He put the bag under his bed. He got his laptop and disconnected from the internet, returned the laptop to its satchel and put it on the floor inside his wardrobe. He turned off the power points in his room, except for his bedside lamp. He gathered his shoes and put them in a garbage bag, ready to burn on the bonfire. Outside, he felt frost forming on the grass between his toes and he felt the dampness soaking into the hems of his jeans. He looked into the fire.

'Nother log'll do 'er, Rene said.

Markus said he'd get it.

Y'got no shoes on.

S'alright.

Elba said, Let him be, Ren. The sangria stuck to her cheeks when she said, Shoes make no difference now. Markus felt more strongly than ever the desire to lose himself in an alternative identity, just as she had. Rene, his face shadowy from the flickering flame, smiled tight and walked away to get another log for the fire. Markus began burning all his shoes, starting with his Blundstones.

The next morning, the bonfire was smouldering and its streaky-white smoke sailed upward into the ironbark canopies above the driveway. There were galahs squabbling over roosting room in the branches, or perhaps the birds were complaining at the smoke. Beneath them, Rene and Markus re-laid straw and replaced geraniums — the first of his father's attempts to return to normal, though these actions would slowly become an invisible leash to keep Markus close. Rene showed Markus how the geraniums flowered: the unassuming flower heads broke open to reveal a delicate flesh-pink flower, which would deepen to a tangerine.

The depth of winter shallows into summer. Markus goes for a walk, passing by his old high school. The tall gum trees around frame it. And standing before that place, he feels he's grown, not up, but away. And not away from that place mentally, but rather away from *place* physically. This place: Narioka.

In year eight or nine his then PE class, called Individual Activities, spent four weeks of first term doing water sports. That means we piss on each other, one of the boys said, and the whole group had laughed. Where's Georges, said another of the boys, he'd be a slut for it. They laughed again, one of them mimicking holding his cock and pretending to piss into the water. Grayson said, Water aerobics is old people's swimming. He'd been standing erect, hands on his hips and a dip in his back: a dip that urged Markus to sink his head in its cradle (like when Grayson would lie down beside the footy oval and rest his head on his arms and his body looked as if it were the perfect place to sleep). Markus watched Grayson watch the water, and saw the crystal-blue reflection dancing in Grayson's brown eyes. Markus stops himself there, aware of the potential disaster of fairy-tale happiness. Cut. Cut. Cut back to the core.

When he gets home from this walk, the ABC is playing reruns of the first season of *Dance Academy*. He has watched it each week previous and now he watches each episode again. Rene and Elba have left him quite alone since his sentencing — they're waiting for the legal papers to come back to see where they've set up his community service. While they wait, one's working and the other is lunching with the girls. At dinner the other night, there was some talk of his twenty-first birthday: his plans, their plans etc. Markus had said nothing. A birthday's not what it once was. For now, he settles in on the couch, blanket over him. Tells himself he has a dancer's body and that this body can leap and soar.

The *Leader*'s on the coffee table. He'd stopped reading the articles about the railway construction saga when the editor had started placing them beyond the crossword. The latest edition reports that due to financial difficulties elicited by drought, the rail project is on hold, of course. Drought this and drought that. It isn't only the absence of water; it sucks life not only out of the land but also from opportunity.

Cat's sitting on the windowsill scratching at the glass, which distracts Markus. Cat meows and starts scratching its claw harder. Markus groans, rolls off the couch, and sways over on all fours. He catches sight of a blur outside, rubs an eye, and when it refocuses he sees a slim, brown-fur cat slink away into the plains-grass paddock. Cat turns its head up, meows. Markus pats it. Cat purrs and slumps off.

After he's folded the blanket over the back of the couch, Markus finds Cat in his bedroom, sleeping on top of the poetry piled at the foot of the bed. Markus taps on his lamp. The light's beautiful and enough. He strips his bed sheets and moves the things that'll get in the way, like his pedestal fan. He vacuums his mattress and his bedside table and the floor and the curtains and the roof. When he's done, he gets a bucket of steaming water. Washes the walls and the door and the window. Goes out the front door and splashes the dirty water into a wild-looking geranium. The liquid drips off the leaves. He remakes his bed. He puts his four pillows in pairs, diagonally beside each other, at the top of the bed. He replaces the pedestal fan. He takes down from the walls the faded Aquaman posters. Opens the curtains, and a cool breeze puffs the lace behind the curtains into his body. It's a little before six — the sky is cyan, pink clouds, and a tinge yellow-green.

—

Elmyra opens the door to her house. She'd called him up while he was contemplating the clouds. She'd asked him over. Her shoulders curl inward when she sees him.

He didn't bring anything — no gift, no card, no flowers — because, as he was rushing out the door to come over here, a vague thought had crossed his mind: *sentimental gestures won't close this gap.*

They'd found Mrs Robinson, dead, sitting in the front seat of her old Falcon. Apparently, she'd driven through the Country Club to the back of the faux island, along its jutting mass, down the bank, and out into the middle of the empty Lake. She'd parked there. Exposed. And hot, very hot inside a closed-up car. The engine was running, and by now there was a hose taped to the exhaust.

Elmyra told him on the phone, in a stream of rapid word-vomit, that she's blu-tacked to her mother's door a flimsy-plastic *danger do not enter* sign. She said she got it from the cheap shop in town, the same place she got her plastic crucifix.

And now, alone in the house, she doesn't invite Markus in with words; rather, it's her eyes that draw him in. The activity inside, suspended momentarily to answer a knock at the door, distracts him from the weight of the situation. A kettle lost in a wild, boiling roar, quietening. Piles of clothes systematically laid out on the kitchen table — dirty, clean, and folded. Dotted between, and spilling out onto the kitchen bench nearby, are vases with flowers and cards embossed in looped script that fails to express the *deepest sympathy* it purports.

I didn't bring anything, he says. He stops to let her pass.

She's close behind him, not looking at him. She runs one of her hands, fingers splayed, through her soft, long hair as she passes by him. Her scent is numb, sleepy. She takes down two mugs from a kitchen overhead cupboard and then looks at him.

It's not ice or glass or any other clichéd glaze in her eyes; it's exhaustion.

I'll get it, he says.

She shrugs, returning to the table to fold the clean and dried clothes.

Markus drops a spoonful of instant into each mug. He notices that the clothes she's washed, all of the clothes, are her mother's clothes. He knows this because the fabric's cut and the patterned intensity of these clothes are not as exact or as fine as what he knows Elmyra prefers. He lightens the coffee with milk, and offers a mug to her. She appraises it and continues folding.

She stops when she comes to a white shirt. Tightens the fabric between her hands.

You okay?

There's a stain.

He lifts his chin, trying to peer to where her gaze is fixed. He says, You can wash it again, yair? Elba makes me use this—

Fuck, she spits. She drops the shirt. She runs a hand through her hair, combing it back.

What's wrong? he says, though as the words leave him, *they* sound wrong.

I'm fucken hopeless is what's wrong.

That's not—

Enough, she cuts him off. She moves past him, opens a drawer and takes out a permanent marker. Across the room, where she opens the door to her mother's room. The plastic *danger* sign falls down.

Fuck, he breathes. He sets down his coffee and follows after her.

Elmyra's cleaned Mrs Robinson's room, and packed away the knickknacks into a few small cardboard boxes. Only a bed, stripped of its sheets, and two bedside tables remain. Elmyra crawls on her hands and knees to the middle of her mother's mattress. She uncaps the permanent marker, biting the cap off with her teeth. Still. Then, she begins scrawling. The nib scratches across the thin threads of her mother's bare bed. Catching and breaking away, catching again. Her hand moves steadily across the mattress, swipes back towards the middle to continue writing.

She jerks upright; her knees depress the mattress as if to engulf her body. She throws the permanent marker at the wall and falls in on herself. She stays side-on, lying across the words she's written.

Markus squats beside the bed and rests his chin on

top of the mattress. She's looking at him, and he at her.

She whispers, I'm sorry.

He smiles. He stands. Helps her to her feet. He takes her to the bathroom and tells her, I'll stay here while you shower. He waits to hear the rush of water before going back to her mother's bedroom. He picks up the 'danger' sign from the floor, chucks it on the mattress, and closes the door behind him. He walks back down the hallway and sits beside the bathroom door.

When she comes out sometime later, her body's sweaty, red, and she smells of honeysuckle and lemon myrtle. He takes her to her own bedroom. When she's sunk beneath her bed's flower canopy, safe under the heavy doona, he sits at her dresser and waits until she's asleep. She's breathing heavily. He turns to the three mirror panes on the dresser: three of him look back from three different angles. He plays with the glass perfume bottles. When he lifts them, they leave clean circles in the dust that's settled. He moves them around, their vibrant tones clinking into each other. This is where she used to become Marilyn.

A few days later, he decides to revisit Elmyra. He's not heard from her. Buff had messaged him and said she'd set a manky mattress on fire in her front yard. Markus wrote his response straight away and then waited an hour to send it. He'd said: *the mattress isn't the point*.

Buff responded within a minute: *exactly u soft cock*.

Markus imagines Elmyra sinking into a bathtub of slow-moving steaming water. Not drowning, just resting beneath the surface while a candle burns fire into the room. He sends back to Buff: *have you seen her*.

everyday u?

For a moment Markus wants to respond with *no she has you* but he doesn't.

On the day he has chosen, a high sun waits for him. He tugs up his polo's collar. No wind. The canopied drive gives shelter. Toward the end of the driveway, he heads over to the orange geraniums, from which he picks full-flowering blooms and three other fine stems with unbloomed buds. He jumps in the empty potholes in the road to town and smiles and laughs and wishes Grayson were here. And that there was rain. Blue. Water to turn the potholes into tiny lakes. A car with its lights on full-beam gains distance. He's looking at the twinkle they make in the heat wave, liquid rising off the road's surface.

If I stay here, it's almost as if none of what has happened ever happened at all. If I stay still. As if all is normal and continual and eternal, like the arching emptiness of the dogged sunlight whipping across the surface at the public pool. Only the pool's waterless. Looking past the car's headlights flashing—

Move, dickhead!

Markus stumbles onto the gravel at the side of the road and the deep-twilight-blue car speeds on behind him. He looks at the geraniums he's picked for Elmyra, and throws them into the tall wild oats growing between the side of the road and the fenced-off paddock at his left. He can't give her flowers; he needs a gesture bigger than petals and stamens and unopened buds.

That's when he gets a call from Georges, which distracts him completely from Elmyra. Because the rippling water returns, unrevealing and dazzling: Georges's eyes. The blue that's been seeping into his vision has been there since last time. Last time, the pearly-white circling Georges's blue was tarnished by thin red capillaries that'd blown, and which wriggled like the vibrant roots of seaweed. Back then, in the pub as 'Otis' played, Georges had said that he was rooted because he'd driven from the city late at night to get to Narioka in time for Grayson's funeral. This time, years later, Georges says he's won a wanky award in the city and that Narioka Council's asked him to bring some artwork for the country folk. For inspiration (and to scoff at).

He says to Markus that it'd be nice if they could catch up. Yair.

Georges says, I get the feeling much has changed and no one's sat drunken in a bar and reviewed the progress.

—

Wind's cold and comes through Markus's thinning jumper, which he's had since he was in year six and that nineteen-year-old cricketer from Manchester (UK) came to play for a season. Markus had heard Manchester fucking a girl from the pub into uncontrolled moans — both hers and his. Markus knows stories of girlfriends wearing items of their boyfriends' clothes, like the girl from the pub the next morning was wearing one of Manchester's shirts with the word 'OBEY' across her breasts. In the days before Manchester was to fly back to the UK, Markus had snuck into his room and stolen a clean-smelling brown jumper out of the tallboy. It seemed like the only thing he could do to maintain his infatuation with Manchester, because, even though Manchester had never laid a finger (or any other body part) on him, Markus wanted to, just like the girl from the pub, feel close to him. Markus is wearing that jumper today. It is old and thinning, but it still fits him, and something this old and from another time is hard to throw away.

There's a seat across from Markus where Georges will sit.

The emptiness of the chair and its potential makes him recall how, in year ten, Buff said he'd gone to a Nine Inch Nails concert in the city and that it wasn't lame to line up after the gig for Ternt/Kent/Trent to sign his CD. CDs, Grayson had said as if they were as ancient as paper and pen. Who on earth buys CDs? And Buff had said nothing. Something he'd been unaware of had been brought to his attention.

Markus shakes his head and looks down the street. Silly stuff. The wind disarms him. His thoughts are promising.

Seeing someone you've not seen for years is like regaining a part of yourself you hadn't realised you'd lost, or like finding money in the washing. Markus realises this as soon as Georges hugs him. They come together, and Georges makes a quiet joke about being the only 'two' in Narioka. As they hug, Georges's biceps press firm against Markus.

They break apart.

Markus says, You got fit. He laughs.

There's like an expectation that I have a fit body now, Georges says. And I like to prove them wrong.

How so?

There's this club in St Kilda, says Georges, maybe it's the crystal, maybe the beat, but all the guys get down to their jockstraps. Mostly it's hairy-fucker bears with beer guts and sweaty chests. He pauses. It's actually quite repulsive.

Is that why you do it?

To be repulsive? No, Markus. Spartan strength doesn't armour you. Nor does a beer gut and hairy chest. Georges winks. The sweat is what gives you away. He pauses and takes a sip of water. He says, I've been at the movies with Elmyra and Cecily. *Gatsby*. Fucken thing ran longer than expected. The man wouldn't die. D'you know it makes me really sad that he didn't want to leave Daisy. He hums to the music playing over the café's PA above them. He says, I loved *Gatsby* since the first time we read it at school. I know I wasn't the only one.

Markus pours himself a glass of water, to which Georges raises his own in a cheers. I reread it recently, Markus says. Found it a bit Baroque.

Isn't that the way of love?

Markus shrugs. Runs his finger around the rim of his glass. Says, What have you been doing the last few years? I didn't hear from you in between.

And I didn't hear from you, Georges says. Mostly? Mum and I go to gallery openings, and eat way too much food. I'm sure people thinks it's lame we spend so much time together, but she did push me out into this world. And, honestly, it's so much more meaningful spending time with her than with some uptight little fairy that only wants a fuck.

Markus tries to play it cool. That can't be all that bad.

Don't get me wrong — I don't mind the sex, but it's so tedious sometimes, and I'd much prefer to do things I enjoy with people I enjoy being around.

You've been busy then?

Sure, Georges says curtly. And you?

Markus looks into his glass, then up and around as he says, Just been here, I guess.

You guess?

Markus shrugs. You've lived here. You know what it's like.

Sure.

Anyway, says Markus. I wanted to say that I liked your exhibition.

Before they met up here, Markus had popped into the Town Hall where the exhibition was. An old lady handed him a booklet, printed on A4 paper and folded in half. It had the titles of each of the paintings and a short description; Markus had thrown it away. They were big canvases, ceiling-height in the old school hall and coloured black, white, and grey. None of them were framed. It was as if they each bled over their individual edges and grew into each other. They were sketch-like oil paintings, mostly of men: some naked, some clothed, some together, some alone. There was nothing provocative or progressive, and Markus had only been able to tell that they were men because he'd been looking hard enough through the restless paint-strokes, which Georges's deliberate hand had seemingly placed in an attempt to censor the truth. They made Markus smile. He wanted to get in between the layers of colour, where the tones shifted and changed and intermingled. They each seemed so full that he felt like if he stood closer, he'd breathe in what he hasn't accepted in himself.

Georges asks, What did you think?

Markus says, They're better than the ones you did in high school.

That's because I've given up trying to explain myself, Georges says. Cold War Kids, y'know, dancing like a martyr.

It softens Markus to hear him mention Cold War Kids.

Georges says, It's a shame I have to go early in the morning. I have to pack the exhibition away. He says, You should come to the big smoke sometime.

Markus replies, One day.

You know when we were in high school and all those boys used to make fun of me? Hearing this said aloud shocks Markus, who fumbles for an explanation, a defence of himself. Georges holds up a hand. You had your own shit to deal with, he says. This is about me. For a moment, Georges is very serious, but then he smiles and his smiling mouth drifts into his words. At the time, my father got sick and I watched him get sicker and sicker, as I started to hate myself more and more because of what those boys were saying, doing, to me. I was cutting myself, taking drugs, crying. And one day when my dad was still at home, he heard me crying.

Markus can't look at him directly.

Dad comes in, coughing, these massive fucken black bags under his eyes. Sits beside me and says, *what are yer doin', mate?* I think he knew that I knew what he meant, even though I said I didn't, because the next thing he says is, *everyone's a cunt, some worse than others, trick is don't let the real bad ones tell yer any different.* I nodded, pretending that I still didn't know he knew his son was a little queer.

But I'm—

Shouldn't matter what I am, Markus, or what I'm not.

What does it matter then?

It matters because 'one day' will get away from you. And here, in Narioka, especially.

The wind blows up from the paddocks outside town and makes Markus's jumper flap against his body and his fringe blow into his eyes. Each time he wipes his hair away, he catches a different aspect of the view before him: the skate park; eucalypts; a finished plate of dinner. None fit together. Except Georges. There's that urge toward him, which has now reshaped itself into Markus wanting Georges to pick him up.

Georges studies Markus, and then asks, You had a twenty-first? I figured my invite just got lost in the mail. An innocent smile indicates a joke.

Markus says, My twenty-first kinda got lost in everything else.

It would've been nice to celebrate. Not everyone gets to.

Maybe. Y'know, things get in the way, and then Elmyra's mother …

Georges doesn't know.

Mrs Robinson topped herself.

No.

El didn't say anything at the movies?

Georges shakes his head. Or Cec. He looks at the pattern in the pavement. The entire movie and neither of them ...

Markus shrugs and says, I think she's enjoying the space.

That's vulgar, Markus, really.

And Markus reminds Georges that Elmyra had cared for her mother since year eight, cared for her like trying to cure a disease.

Whether or not Elmyra is enjoying the new space created by her absent mother, the next morning, as Markus is hanging washing out on the line, he can't quite believe he'd said it. Perhaps seeing Georges had made him say more than he'd anticipated; perhaps what he said was, purely, an explanation for how he feels about Elmyra and her mother. He's hanging undies by their corners with one peg. The Hills Hoist's wire is beginning to fray. This whole time he's avoided reconnecting with his oldest friend because he hasn't felt he's had the right way to go about it. *Fuck it.* Inside, he tosses the washing basket into the laundry trough. Into his room, where he dons a hoodie and his orange Vans.

He ducks out the back door, walking through the paths between the veggie beds, toward the shed. He opens the gun cabinet and takes out his father's gun. He collects two shots, and two shots only, before heading around the front of the house, to Rene's ute. He places the gun behind the driver's seat. Takes a moment before he gets in. Elmyra swirls like a wide skirt through his hesitation.

Markus drives to Elmyra's house. Kills the engine when he arrives. Vibrations still tingling in him as he walks up the front path and knocks on door. She doesn't answer, of course, so he jumps the side fence and goes around the back. The sliding door is open. Sitting beside the fruit bowl on her dining-room table is a postcard he found in St Vinnies years and years ago. Light reflects off the Pink Lady apples in the bowl, giving the card in a rosy glow. He'd given it to her one birthday. It has on its front a picture of Marilyn Monroe, without make-up and looking directly at the viewer.

El, he calls into the space. You in here? He goes to her bedroom.

She's sleeping inside. Her head almost covered entirely by the doona, in a cocoon of her own making. Beside her sleeps Buff Burrows. *Immovable.* Of course he is. His back's not covered by the doona. Exposed.

El, he whispers so as not to wake Buff. He places his hand on her shoulder. Wake up, El.

She stirs.

El.

She recoils, takes a moment to assess. The fuck, Markie? she mumbles.

He places a finger over his mouth, glares at Buff beside her.

We're sleeping.

Were, he corrects.

What?

C'mon, he whispers, heading over to her wardrobe. He carefully opens the doors and looks at the rainbow of colour inside.

Where are we going? He sees in her tri-fold mirror that she's stretching under the covers. He sees as she rolls over to Buff and presses her lips to his temple.

Business to do, he says.

Huh.

He selects a dress. Turns and shows it to her.

Remind me to never let you pick my outfit. She gets out of bed and pushes him from the room.

He sits in the lounge, watching the ABC, as she gets ready. She comes out dolled-up as Marilyn. He smiles.

What? she says.

Marilyn.

She's picking her fingernails. She says, Fuck off, Markus.

He flicks the TV off and takes her by the hand. At the ute, he helps her up into the cabin because she's wearing heels. He gets in behind the wheel.

You right? she says, fixing her make-up in the visor's mirror.

Yair, he says taking hold of the wheel, yair I am. He

starts the engine and drives them out to the Lake, pulling up near to the edge.

Fuck off, Markie, she says.

Wait.

You can't be serious, she says, looking out the passenger window. Why bring me *here*?

He reaches behind the driver's seat and pulls out the shotgun.

She laughs, You've fucken lost it.

No, it's right here in my hand. He gets out. She follows, complaining that her heels are sinking in the sand. At the edge, they stand, perhaps near to where they'd once stood in their bathers, back when the Lake was full. He can't remember. Nor can she. She's staring out, probably at the place where her mother's car was found.

She says, I haven't been out here since it happened.

He's holding the gun's barrel pointed to the empty Lake. He's not sure how they got to Mrs Robinson through the tangle of overgrown weeds lining the Lake's bed. Further across, on the faux island projecting into this mess, the rabbits at the edge of the Lake skitter and dart up the bank into the longer grass. Two of them. Fat. Free. Feral.

What are we doing here? Elmyra whines a little. She stretches out her arms high above her head. I just want to go home.

He points the gun toward the pair of rabbits. Markus

had never let his father teach him how to shoot. So he says to her, You take the first shot. You were always good at clay target. He holds out the gun for her; she is hesitant, her head dipping to the weapon then back up to him.

Then, with a firm, distinct grip, she takes it.

He says, Keep an eye out and wait.

You never learnt how to shoot, she says, so don't tell me what to do. She places the gun's butt against her shoulder, assumes her stance as if professional. Your turn next.

But before he can protest, one of the rabbits hops down onto the bank on the faux island, slowly and very cautiously. The second follows, hopping over to its mate. Elmyra releases the safety, cocks the barrel, and shoots. Part of the head, the brain, of the first rabbit spatters onto the second.

Fuck, Markus says.

She snaps open the barrel and says, Rabbits are a lot easier than clays. She puts out her hand for the second round, which he pulls out of his pocket and hands to her. She loads the gun with ease, snapping the barrel back into place. Your turn, she says.

He shakes his head.

For fuck's sake. She grabs his arm. Like this. She presses the gun's butt into his shoulder and takes him by the hand, telling him where to hold it.

There's no rabbit to shoot, he says.

The second one'll come back down to check on its

mate, she says. Rabbits are dumb, they always do. Don't put your finger on the trigger until you're ready to shoot. I'll get everything; you just shoot when I say.

Just as she said would happen, the second rabbit steps out of the grass and comes down to the side of the first. It sniffs the tattered remains.

Aim.

Markus says, Fuck, under his breath, really quietly.

Put your finger on the trigger, she says.

And he does.

Now.

II.

On the day

One eye of the young man Markus Bello opens from some waking dream. There's his mobile phone's final ring before silence. As he shifts across the bed to pick it up, it rings again.

Get up t' the top paddock. Brute's here t' get some wood, Rene says. And don't forget the axe.

After some extended moments to himself, Markus dresses and goes down the hall to the open-plan living area. He finds last night's leftovers — empty beer stubbies — and his mate Grayson, who is shirtless and sleeping on the couch. Markus leaves Gray there and exits the house. He gets the axe from the shed and, swinging its cutting blade through the air, he footslogs the corrugated road toward, not quite to, the cliffs at the edge of Rene's farm.

The sun's been long up and a few clouds loiter. Maybe it'll rain in the arvo. The plains grass Rene's planted sways and rustles as if material. From the barbed-wire fence hang the stiff carcasses of three foxes. Wild oats, which Rene's keen to keep outside his paddocks, grow on the outside of the fence and bend against the foxes' dried-out noses. The oats' shorter stalks touch Markus's legs, and their seed-heads snatch his socks and then flick upright, trembling.

Rene and Brute stand in waist-high plains grass on the inside of the fence. They wear the same clothes, their arms over their chests, legs apart, leaning a little back. Beside the men, on the outside of the fence in the thin band of wild oats, is a dark squiggle stretching skyward: a red ironbark, whose higher twigs retain thin leaves.

Markus says, You could've used a chainsaw.

Use ya head, says Rene. The bats'll die from a chainsaw. And I won't be doin' it.

If Rene was worried about the bats, he wouldn't cut down the tree. But Rene said. And what Rene says, goes.

Don't look at me for help, Brute says. Bad backs, mate. His pointing finger moves between himself and Rene. We're not getting any younger, neither.

Markus's grip tightens on the smooth axe's haft as he approaches the tree. The steel head above his body reverts, slams down and bites into blackish bark. *Thunk.* He grunts, knocks at the trunk again. *Thunk.* His head pangs from his hangover and might explode.

He limp-wristed or what? Brute jokes.

Thunk. Chips of wood pirouette and pass Markus's

eyes and body. Vibrations through his lungs and heart as if he's tumbling.

Rene starts to speak with a muffled voice, says, He was shit-carted last night — *thunk* — disappeared.

Yair right, Brute says. Buff didn't go.

Thunk.

Rene says, His mate couldn't stand — *thunk* — on my couch, everywhere.

Thunk.

Boys'll be — *thunk* — at their age, Brute says, chicks were hangin' off — *thunk* — that girl, Robinson?

Thunk.

Thunk.

Thunk.

Now ya showin' off, Rene says. And ya not doin' a very good job of it. He comes out of the paddock and offers his hand. He begins hacking the remaining cut himself and says, If ya want somethin' done …

The tree cracks and falls and thuds onto the earth.

Brute comes outside the paddock to kick the fallen tree. Good thing ya gettin' rid a this one, Ren. Next t' no water this year. Not with those cunts upstream.

It's goin' back into the system, Rene says. The Basin Plan — enough for the farms and enough to keep the river systems healthy. He hands the axe back to Markus and tells him to chop the rest into logs. He reminds Brute that the withholding of water's only for a year.

Brute spits and says, Fuck yair, an' we're left a dustbowl. It's fucken overregulated, Ren. An' the allocation we get's piss-weak.

What allocation? Rene offers lightly.

Markus chops the limbs into pieces. With a Blundstone kick, one of the logs rolls to the bare ground at the side. Catching his breath, he stands upright. He rests the axe and turns to the morning light spiking over the cliff's lip behind them. He's never been over the escarpment. It protrudes solidly. He looks past the men. One of them moves, and his silhouette blocks the bold beams.

Rene says, What is it ya little friend does?

Grayson? says Markus. Works at IGA.

Rene's silhouette swats his forearm for flies. Y'know what I mean. What's he wanna do?

Make music.

Brute says, He's dreamin'.

Markus turns away. He forms his fingers into a fist, tightens and unclenches.

Where you been? Grayson's awake, sitting up on the couch. He scratches his armpit and hugs himself.

The telly's playing a *Skins* DVD.

Markus says, holding up the log, Using my head.

Yair, dickhead, says Rene. Except it's gunna be forty-five t'day. He scruffs his son's hair. His hands are as rough, dry, and calloused as the land he lives and farms on. Right, youse boys. I'm havin' a shower, then I'll take y'home. He looks at Grayson.

Grayson nods.

Rene exits into the master bedroom, yelling out, Be ready when I am.

Yair, easy fixed. Grayson puts on his shirt. He stands, tousles his hair, stretches his arms, and pulls his jeans over his undies: the humblest of the not-famous warriors adorns his armour.

While Rene's in the shower, Markus bids his mate to escape. And they do. They decide to go to the public pool, because heat. Markus, being sober-er, drives Grayson's car, saying, You'll be over the limit. Grayson sings to the radio, Lisa Mitchell, as they head through the drying-out land toward Narioka. Anything on the inside of Grayson wouldn't have ever made it outside if not for the music he loves. It's like having someone say what you wanna say, Grayson says, and you take that and pretend it's not what you feel. Lisa Mitchell was on Australian Idol when we were in like year six. She grew up in Albury. Won awards. Plays at festivals, even had songs in the triple j Hottest 100. I'm playin' some of her stuff tonight, says Grayson.

In town, they pass the newsagent, chemist, and the teenage mothers smoking rolled cigarettes and drinking Red Bull out front of the Chicken Ranch.

—

Standing in the mid-section of the public pool, the water's ice-blue and cool on Markus's skin. The sky's ceramic-white from the flaky smoke of the wheat stubble that's burning outside of town. Sun tries splintering through this haze. St Augustine grass (*Stenotaphrum secundatum*) beside the concrete path, which runs around the outside of the pool, is bottle-green and blue-shaded by a few mature ironbarks: the result of illegal night-watering, no doubt. Markus looks at the shallow end. He wants to touch Grayson: the grace and the body stir him, the face. Grayson from last night, when he and Markus broke in to the pool: how victorious *that* Grayson had been, while half-in-the-bag. Grayson standing as if he's caught sight of something he's never seen before. He's upright with his hands on his hips and an arch in his back, his head down with his eyes trained on the water.

A younger boy, the youngest of the Drumanure kids, brushes past Grayson into the water and splashes below him.

Grayson shifts his hands from his hips, slides them quicker up and crosses them over his chest. Biceps bulge, perfect footy pose. Except he's never played footy. He moves down a step, releases himself, and steps down once more. Mouth open, an involuntary, Ha, escapes before he duck-dives into the shallows. His body wavers beneath the water like a school of a million shimmering fish, wavers and reassembles when he comes up for air.

Water purls off his face, and he wipes sodden shaggy hair across his forehead. So clear is it all: the endless pool, his eyes, the beads of water curling about his exposed skin and the sky above reflecting itself off the surface. Grayson is the island, and this is overwhelming for Markus: his proximity to making landfall.

Fuck, it's fresh, ay, says Grayson.

It's alright once you're used to it.

You'd know. Grayson blows water from his lips. You're here every mornin'.

Nah, I come a bit earlier than this. You've held me up, Gray. Markus pushes the surface with his hand. A tiny wave unfurls toward Grayson.

Four years back was when Markus had caught first sight of land. Grayson was some other kind of island then, gliding across the silvery lake on a kneeboard. Rene reminded them how lucky they'd been to see the Lake full and to swim, nah, to kneeboard on it! Nearby the Lake is the water tower that everyone pretends is the lighthouse from *Round The Twist*. Markus had felt like a freak standing on the Lake's shore, blown by the wind, hot in his wetsuit, and conscious of the outline of his cock in the tight material. He'd been the last to enter the so-called swell. Crayfish (*Euastacus armatus*), yabbies (*Cherax destructor*), freshies (*Crocodylus johnstoni*). Rarely, rarely down here with freshies, someone had said. C'mon, get in — yer can't just stand there watchin'! Those critters were excuses, though. He had, in fact, sighted land, his island, in the beam of that fake lighthouse.

Annoyed at himself, he slips beneath the pool's surface and sinks and lets his back touch the bottom. He looks upward. The sunlight whips on the surface. A pinkish garble reels at the corner — a child, perhaps. A child, perhaps, who's pin-dropped beside him. He ignores, or tries to ignore, the rippling image. He focuses on how his body's unenthusiastic here … His eyes open wider and he turns upright to meet the child's face. The child paddles his arms beside himself to keep his body below. They mark time. They go through it not around it. They puff their cheeks and round their eyes, somehow it'll make them see clearer. Which it does. Adjustment. The child is Grayson. From the moment he saw the figure pin-drop, Markus knew it was Grayson, with stubble over his white cheeks and over his neat chin, and a few dots of acne-scar discolouration. Gray looks like a puffer fish frightened to inflation. It's laughable. The air bubbles out from their lungs and chuckles to the surface. Markus puts his feet down on the semi-slimy bottom and follows his bubbles upward. Life returns: aahahahaha, splishing barefootedness, and dank wet concrete cutting into the actual grassy knoll.

Markus sees, as he turns and leans over the side of the pool, the lawn pegged with naked skins slapping their surfaces with sunscreen. triple j comes tinny through the PA: 'Hero', by Family of the Year. He stretches the muscles in his neck.

Grayson leans beside him; their skins brush as he scratches his stubble. And with the scratching, the child becomes a young man. Tryin' to get away? He stops scratching and places his hands, palms down, atop the pool's overflow grate.

Markus watches the clear weather swirl in the ripples rushing over each of his hands and down into the dark grate, to be regurgitated later.

There's some light pinning the water beads on Gray's collarbone. He sniffs. Too bad.

Toward the shallow end, the Drumanure family is playing with a wailing Vortex.

Grayson turns to look, and Markus glances over his own shoulder.

The youngest Drumanure kid yells, It's mine, with a voice on the edge of manhood: its pitch is undecided, and then breaks.

That sucks, Grayson says. He lifts himself up onto the side of the pool. He faces the water.

Young Drumanure, with the Vortex, is yelled at by his father. Markus turns to the grassy knoll behind Grayson and sees the other Drumanure son: the boy they used to go to school with and whom Markus once threw a mouldy sanga at. This Drumanure (left school to be a butcher) is sitting up, knees drawn, and looking down at the arse and bare skin of the girl beside him: is that Cecily? Markus pretends it isn't; with her on her belly, and her face buried in her arms and under a hat, it's hard to tell. Elder Drumanure and Maybe-Cecily are in dappled shade. Several noisy miners (*Manorina melanocephala*) sit on top of the more-than-six-foot cyclone wire fence encasing the pool. Behind the fence is the north end of Melville Street, which runs beside the pool complex and today — a Sunday — the road is empty. Parallel to Melville Street are the rose gardens, with their centrepiece a replica tar-coloured steam locomotive. The gardens are silent and the blooms nod in the breeze. The tributary creek from the Lake, which cuts through town a little further south, is empty on the other side of these gardens.

Grayson said another time, when he was giving Markus a collection of Platonic dialogues (As a joke, Markus, I don't expect you to read them) that a conversation's an amazing thing. You can pull it out of nowhere. Make it into whatever. Say whatever. Lie. Tell the absolute truth. Myth make.

Elder Drumanure has his back turned against all this. He has an orange towel wrapped around his shoulders; he is filled with potential.

Younger Drumanure, now without the Vortex, comes and sits on the grass in front of Markus and beside his brother. Younger Drumanure looks to Elder Drumanure, to Maybe-Cecily and then away as he laughs and hides his face. Elder Drumanure spins, Oi, and throws a bottle at his brother, telling him to, Grow a fucken pair.

Gray. Markus nods toward the other boys.

But Grayson goes on staring at the water. He is distant. A distance Markus has been trying to make up ever since that camping trip the two of them took back in high school.

When the two of them were alone, Grayson had wanted to know about what Markus wanted to do, about where Markus wanted to go, and about who Markus wanted to be. And Markus couldn't answer any of it. So the two boys skinny-dipped and went to bed.

That's what Markus remembers.

Grayson in a swag across from him, with his legs and arse covered by a folded back sleeping bag. His shoulder blades lifted and fell. The last of dusk filtered through the tent. Markus had lain on the top of his own sleeping bag, and didn't understand it all. Grayson is the messiest person: his things had been flung, strewn, tossed, and fluttered. A raven (*Corvus coronoides*) had opened its black onyx beak, stretched its tonsils, and declared ahr ahrr ahrrrrr. And inside the tent the noise had echoed in Markus's mind long after the bird had settled again. Towels — wet, dry, dirty — and jocks, socks, shirts, shorts, and shoes remained scattered. That was after year eight, during summer holidays. The Lake was still filled at that stage (not for much longer, it'd turn out). And it was the night that Buff decided to stay. Grayson hadn't told Markus, who was under the impression that Grayson hated Buff. So Markus had been feigning sleep when Buff arrived. Grayson, whispering, cleared a space between his own sleeping bag and Markus's. After the rustling settled, Buff whispered about this girl he'd been texting. She's got a bangin' bod. Markus hadn't heard what Grayson said. But he had heard what Buff replied at length, Shit my rufus is hard. Markus's voice had broken, as if a self-betrayal, in reply when Buff asked, You listenin'?

Dad, why the fuck did ya send him over for? Elder Drumanure yells. He stands. There's no answer. He bounds toward Younger Drumanure, who sprints toward the pool and dives over Markus's head. Elder Drumanure follows. They disappear beneath the wading bodies across the breadth of the pool.

Heroes, Grayson says. He pushes off from the overflow grate. He sinks underneath and comes back up beside Markus, where he started. Spits and says, I wish I was ... I dunno.

Pardon?

I dunno. If I could lose my mind, maybe I'd be happy. Like the people in old people's homes — where I don't know what I want and I'm happy with whatever I get given.

Like dementia? Markus sees the shoreline of the Lake, when it had been full those years ago on the camping trip.

That same trip, Gray had told Markus that he'd lost his virginity. What's it like? Markus had said.

Now, with Grayson standing in the water beside him, Markus asks about Cecily.

Wrestling to the fore in Markus's mind is an image of a victorious Grayson testing the choppy surface of the Lake. He's trying to get to Markus, who wades titan-like beyond the submerged sandbar. Out from the waves, draped in sparkling green weeds and crowned with mustard-coloured stones, Cecily walks up onto the beach. Her eyes are yabby-shell blue, and her skin creamy-smooth like the underbelly of Murray Cod (*Maccullochella peelii*). Grayson'd never told him what losing your virginity is like, and Markus has never imagined a good enough answer to fill the absence.

Hi, boys.

And then here Cecily is. For real. Which upsets Markus, because of how abruptly she appears, though it shouldn't, because it *was* her on the grassy knoll who Elder Drumanure had been leering at. She's standing right there on the concrete footpath before them. Actual, no longer just potential.

Grayson kisses her neck. They walk to get ice-cream.

And furious Markus, with Poseidonic strength, slashes at the water. A sheet of liquid sprays up and lands on Youarang walking past.

The couple comes back.

Grayson hands Markus an orange-flavoured Sunny Boy. Cecily and Grayson each have a waffle cone with a double scoop of cherry. Cecily tries to compensate with, We couldn't decide for you.

Youarang, who's hovering, tells Markus, Don't eat in the pool.

Markus says, Get fucked, and splashes water at him, this time on purpose.

A noisy miner comes down from the fence, stretches a quiet noise in its mouth, as if enquiring. Cecily shoos it with her hand. It jumps back. When her pathetic defence subsides, it waddles even closer.

She waves again. Someone shoot that bloody thing.

Grayson squawks in its direction, and the bird flaps inelegantly away.

They'd survive a nuclear war.

Nah, not even a cockroach can.

Um, yes.

Yair. They can survive the radiation; a direct hit would kill 'em all.

Things aren't meant to be around for too long anyway, says Markus, cutting in.

Well, people aren't meant to live for as long as they do, at least, says Grayson.

Cecily says, Our generation's meant to live to a hundred and fifty.

Nah. They say a thousand.

Who's they?

They. Grayson laughs. Says, If we lived back years ago, we'd already have kids and a wife.

Cecily says, Too soon. Her voice is nasal.

Grayson says, Thank fuck we live now. His voice smoothed out by the ice-cream.

After a pause, Markus says, Why you here early, Cec? You usually come just before closing.

Everyone's here, she says. She tips back her wide-brimmed hat, lowers her Ray-Bans and scans the pool. Bright beams of light reflect across her face. She says, So much skin.

They are quiet.

Markus stands in the water.

Grayson says, I gotta go home. Get shit organised for the gig tonight.

I'm looking forward to it, Markus says.

It's just me an' me guitar. Nothin' great.

Okay.

I hope it works out, Grayson says. Adds something about hating it if he was stuck in Narioka forever, playing shitty gig after shitty gig in its three shitty dying pubs.

I hope you wish for more than that, says Cecily.

Like what?

A proper job, she says.

Grayson pushes Markus's shoulder. Sounds like your old man.

Being in town, Markus heads to Elmyra's. It is, after all, her birthday. *We're twins*, she'd said to him last night at his own birthday party. *A day apart and from different wombs*, he'd reminded her. She'd come to his party dressed as Marilyn singing to Mr President; Markus'd taken off her white-fur jacket to reveal her glittering floor-length dress. He gets to the door of her house. It has a stained-glass motif in it. No answer. He rings her. *Hiya. I'm screening calls. Make it wonderful.* He tells the voicemail he'll come by later.

Down the end of her street he can see cliffs: constant, flat, grey. Today they're shimmying from the heat. It's a pleasant area to look at. Narioka and the Depression, that is. Heading in the opposite direction past the places he'd driven by with Grayson earlier, Markus begins walking home. Out south, the pavement crumbles to hydrophobic-red dirt, and the dirt stitches itself into spiny strands of grasses and weeds; dead, dying, yellowish-grey. Walking beside the laser-ploughed fields — burnt-soil precision cut by some expensive machine — he sees that even the trees, standing near and far as if for some stage set, have been circumscribed. Manufactured and unnatural. Modern farming. Orders barked from dusted lips give way to the rapid put-put-put of truck or helicopter or drone. *It's such a drone.* Now, out on these plains with longer grass and older trees, his pace slows. Sun splinters, lands in the space between objects. Burns his neck and arms. A heat haze keeps its distance. The drooping trees on his father's driveway frame this view, their leaves appearing as black liquid drops that their limbs forbid they drip. Hot and sweaty and sunburned, he wades through the house and into the bathroom. He wets his face and hair.

Rene rediscovers him, i.e., finds that his son and his son's best mate ran away and now one has returned. His father says, Ya lucky y'didn't get bit by a brown snake.

I didn't want to put you out.

Markus, that's not ... His father pauses. As if it's safer, he tells him to go catch mice for Snake.

Markus grabs an empty bucket and heads to the shed. He could be making Rene proud. He's thankful Rene's not here to see his inadequacy. The mice Markus catches he'll release when Rene's not around. He hunts near his broken motorbike, near the prep table where his father grows seedlings, near the back and behind what they no longer need or have hidden in order for it to be forgotten. He follows squeaks and captures carefully in his hands warm, shaking mice (*Mus musculus* meaning 'little thief'). Their black eyes don't seem to register him. There used to be a dam out back. It's still there, though bone-dry now and filled with windmill grass (*Chloris truncate*). When the dam was full, they'd yabby in it, and he'd drop in rail stones and watch the corrugated ripples. The stones plunking to and resting on the dark bottom never felt the tremors they made.

When he gets back to the house, he hears two deep voices, deeper than his own, in the cavern of the open-plan area. They resonate and spill out into the hall. Markus removes his boots. As he comes down into the room, Rene's hand slips away from Buff's back. They're standing near the dining table. Rene's offered Buff a beer and refrained from drinking himself.

His father clears his throat and says, I hafta get some things from town for Elba. His solid eyes at Markus, who reckons the man'd wanted to do this when he'd planned to take Grayson back earlier.

Rene has rules. *Don't drink and drive. Finish the food on your plate. Leave whatever drinks you take to someone's house there. Go outside. Kitchen benches are for glasses not arses. Don't cry in front of anyone. How do you know you don't like it if you've never tried it? A proper job's a proper income. Labour's the backbone of society.* Rules that are uttered moments before you're about to break one. They aren't like the rules that other boys have. Buff has a 9.30pm curfew. The Youarang boy (so Markus found out through Buff) has a pocket-money system that decreases by a few bucks every time he wets the bed. Grayson has to leave the house at least once on the weekends. Rene could say, *Can y'feed Cat?* Markus would say, *In a minute.* And Rene understands that a minute in Markus's time is anywhere from five minutes to an hour. The job will get done. One rule is odd, though. Markus has never asked why the song

'Fast Car' isn't allowed to play when Rene's in earshot. He's never asked because of the way Rene growls, Turn that fucken music orf. So, when Rene tells Markus to feed the mice he's captured to Snake, Markus knows Rene's punishing him for running off with Grayson's car. He wouldn't've been that much over the limit, but still …

His father leaves after shaking Buff's hand.

Gunna do it? Buff squats next to the bucket and plucks a mouse by its tail. He suspends it in the air in front of his face.

Markus says, Later, picturing releasing the mice when there's no men about.

Pussy. Buff drops the mouse and grabs the bucket. I thought you were all for gettin' rid a pests, said as a statement, not a question. Buff walks behind the couch in the lounge to where Snake's tank is kept. When ya dad says do somethin', ya do it. He slides the glass off the top. Keen for the charity footy match?

I haven't seen it in the paper.

Narht, not goin' in for a coupla weeks yet. Buff smirks. Y'better be ready. He takes the smallest mouse and holds it up to the side of the tank. Coach'll wring ya nuts if ya not.

Snake, within the tank, eyes the mouse.

I'll see.

Buff stands. Ya better do more than see. He drops the mouse inside the tank.

No sooner does the mouse hit the sandy bottom, and

take its first bound, does Snake strike and eat. There's a muffled squeak.

Beauty. Buff turns to Markus and winks. I'll leave the rest to you.

Outside, in the buzz of a kazillion cicadas and the hum of the air-con unit on the roof, the more docile cool morning unfurls into a dragging afternoon. The muscles and bones of Markus's body feel both bound down and restless. He lingers inside the shed, near the back, where the light falls on the engine of his motorbike enough to make the metal look, from the position he squats in, older than it is. He fiddles with tools. The clinking and tinking dulls on the oily rags he's placed around the guts of the toolbox. By bending beside the machine, he's trying to convince Buff that he knows more than words and books and shit that's useless out here. There's a sweating-fruit smell — which he tries to ignore — puffing from somewhere nearby. *Cologne de provincial.* It makes him sick: it's a reminder of high school and of Buff Burrows speaking nearby him. Markus chooses to not quite hear. He downs the tool on the concrete floor. Stands. Grabs a Wrigley's from his chest pocket, hopes its taste will overpower the fruity smell. Offers one to Buff. Narht, is the reply. Markus chews and whacks his now grotty palm on the leather seat. The motorbike creaks. Both young men gravitate toward the shed's entry. They lean with their backs on opposing poles. Fruity smell wafting between him and Buff — what a wanker: immovable, with sweat on his neck and on his nose and talking, staring out of the shed and not listening, even to himself. How much a man. Nobody of seventeen is very serious, but Buff's too mud-stuck to realise.

I started up at the abs, says Buff, y'know, like three years back. We're walking through the kill room an' the boss tells me that the world's fucked, right. Doesn't matter if I slaughter animals. Means nothin'. Life goes on an' shit.

Markus stretches, trying to rid himself of the suffocating drowsiness. Your boss was right.

What d'ya mean?

Nothing gets out alive — what's a few years less of living?

That's a bit rough.

Or realistic.

Buff gets to work on the bike. He says, I'll stick with rough, ay. Bit like this bloody rig, Bellos.

It does the job when it goes.

How often's that? Bent down beside the motorbike, Buff ticks or tocks his tongue against the roof of his mouth. He discards the spanner and uses lock-grip pliers instead. You're a spastic, he says, an' ya call y'self a mechanic's apprentice.

Soon to be a mechanic's apprentice, Markus says.

What d'ya call y'self now?

A cowherd, pastoralist, grazier, I dunno. Out of work.

Yair, right, Buff says.

These are too bucolic, though. Markus laughs by making a sound like he's spat out nothing. Watching Buff, he decides he needs age-appropriate hobbies. Reading doesn't cut it anymore, let alone the poetry sitting at the foot of his bed. Maybe photography. Instagram. Snapchat. He could start a Tumblr and post his own dick-pics #sickcunt #hungaf #iwish.

Buff says he's fixed the motorbike. He comes back to stand against the pole across from Markus.

An engine ripples through the yard. A Jeep churns dust, cuts its engine.

What a fucker. Buff's gazing at the Jeep through his half-closed eyes.

Elba?

Me boss. What a fucker for tellin' me shit like that. I mean, I was fourteen. He sighs.

Elba emerges from the Jeep. She looks around briefly and then sashays into the house through the front door.

Where's she been? Buff says.

Markus says, Alice Springs. Darwin, too.

Hasn't she already been there?

Markus shrugs.

Buff takes out a cigarette. I hate that. His cheeks compress as he sucks the smoke, which soon clouds back past his lips into the dry air. He thrusts a hand down the front of his footy shorts, scratches and readjusts whatever he's packing.

What do you hate?

Travel. Buff drags the ciggie. Exhales the toxins. Dad went to the Alice, he says. Buff removes his hand from his footy shorts. Dad said that every day, fuck, there's coons all over the place, fucken stoned an' spaced. Layin' in the gutter like fucken rubbish. Drags deep, eyes squint. White smoke ribbons up and down in front of him. He says, There's fucken dirt, right, red dirt to the end of the earth. Y'ask Youarang, he'd know about it.

Why's that, Buff?

'Cause, well. Y'know. 'Cause the kid's a ... Buff puts his thumb and index fingers either side of his nostrils. He widens the space the fingers indicate.

You're a cunt, Burrows.

And you're a soft cock.

It doesn't matter where Youarang was born; just like you, he's never left Australia.

Whatever. Buff smokes. Then he nods at Elba's car. Those rigs are a bit gay, seen the fucken telly ads? *I boughta Jeeeep.* Fuck me dead. Buff smokes. When's she an' Ren gettin' hitched?

Markus shrugs. He thinks of the motorbike, and how he starts his mechanic's apprenticeship on Monday coming: another arena in which he will perform his absolute incompetency at labour.

I seen Elmyra earlier, Buff says.

You two have been spending more time together.

Buff nods slow, considered. What of it?

Markus shrugs. Hope you're treating her well.

Fuck you.

I mean it.

What would you know? Buff says. She said you don't bother much anymore. She said somethin' about youse a few days back.

Yair?

(Markus and Elmyra had walked into her room on Wednesday afternoon. It was 43°C, and he'd had sweat sliding down from his back to the top of his arse crack. As he took a seat on her bed, she'd said, Why do we even talk anymore?)

So whatta y'gunna do?

I don't see why I need to do anything.

I can see what she means but.

Markus considers this.

She says ya spend too much time talkin' shit with ya mates. Buff drags his ciggie. With *Grayson*. The way he says Grayson's name, the way he exhales it with the cigarette smoke, is as if he regrets bringing it up. He sips a breath of fresher air, like he's jumped in freezing water. I told her ya fucked in the head. He laughs like it's a joke.

Markus says, I'm not her property. He decides to raise his voice, not too loud, just taking control of the phonemes, and not necessarily because Buff's making him angry: rather, the word 'her' is there to be taken control of.

'Her' is absent and therefore eligible for this.

She didn't mean it like that, Buff says.

There's more that Markus could say. He wants to tell Buff to stop pretending to be such a fucken man — you're Buff Burrows, not Brute.

Buff says, Have y'ever?

What?

Y'know?

There's a *no* because it's the truth, but Markus stifles the *no* with a shrug. Says, It's what everyone else is doing.

Buff smokes.

There's quietness.

The security door of the laundry rattles, slams.

Boys, Elba calls across the yard. Mark. Come inside from the heat. I have lunch.

Buff tosses aside his cigarette butt, squashes it with his boot. He has a deliberate gait; he keeps his eyes trained on the ground as he walks from here to there, as if not to catch sight of the vastness and have thoughts of insignificance.

Inside, Elba sways over. Her orange flamenco skirt swishes, her gold earrings jangle. Her bone-hard arms press into Markus's sides. He releases himself from her hug and sits at the table.

I got you a gift. Elba produces a copper-coloured rock inside a plastic zip-lock bag.

What is it?

Ayers Rock, she says.

Markus sighs. Uluru.

Elba gives him a blank look as she swirls away into the nearby kitchen for a tray of cold meat sangas and a bottle of home-brand fizzy drink to clear their throats.

Buff hogs his share; his fingers wriggle in a proud way. Strangling the bread, which he kinda shoves at his lips before they're opened. White crumbs hang on his short moustache. Markus selects the pickles and ham triangles from the platter. Elba sips her drink, a triangle of sandwich untouched on her plate. Everybody in town knows she's really Samantha. This random correction filters through Markus, unspoken, of course, yet regularly enough that it reaffirms the truth and breaks him out of the fantasy.

After lunch, he and Buff head to the front entry.

Markus says, Thanks for the bike, the help and all. He turns to a fish tank sitting on a side table. Fish darts around the plastic plant inside.

Buff knocks into the wall as he slides his boots on, ticking his tongue again. Who owns that?

Me.

Buff scratches his chin. He says, D'fishes come up for air? He clears his throat. Up to the surface.

Markus says, Fish are made of water, I don't think—

Fish breaks the surface.

Buff flicks on his childish smile. He did it.

So he did.

Buff says, Water looks dirty.

I forget he's up here, Markus says.

Can't blame ya. Buff bends his nose to the glass and taps his finger beside it. Shame about the water. Kinda waste, what with the drought.

It's only a fishbowl full, says Markus.

Buff snorts a glob of mucous into his mouth. He swallows. Dad's pretty much given up on the sheep. Sold three quarters last week.

Sorry to hear.

Nah. Because of those cunts upstream. They oughta be sorry. Dad says they've kept heaps a water back for those fucken wetlands. Birds or some shit, endangered. Shoot the fucken lotta 'em, if y'ask me. He sniffs. You'll be right at the mechanics. Don't need much water for that, ay. Laughs a bit. How's y'old man doin'? He wouldn't say before.

Markus talks about how Rene has that native grass in, seems robust, and the beef cattle are good.

Fucken smart bloke, he is. Too bad he's a Greenie. I'd like to use some a' them for target practice. Don't y'reckon?

Yair nah, he wouldn't like that.

Kiddin', Bellos.

Markus places his hands in his pockets and finds and fiddles with a grass seed at the corner of one. He looks down into Fish's tank. Perhaps it's stagnant in there. Maybe Buff is right; maybe Fish needs to break the surface sometimes. He bends and flicks a switch.

A gentle gurgle sounds in the entry: Fish's filter. Some movement to tell Fish that there's movement beyond what it's made of.

If Grayson knew Buff was here he'd be shitty, but Grayson doesn't need to know. And it's not like Buff's going to tell because Buff doesn't consider the emotions of a situation. Except sometimes he does get a squint around his eyes, which makes you think he's second-guessing his interior.

Buff thrusts a hand down the front of his footy shorts, readjusts. Catch ya at footy soon, mate.

Markus lies across his bed. Brings Grayson's name up in his phone.

Markus: *Hey.*

Grayson: *Hey.*

Markus: *Get the stuff organised?*

Grayson: *Nahh having a sleep.*

Markus: *Did I wake you?*

Grayson: *Yeppp gunna go back to sleep.*

Markus: *My bad. Sleep well.*

Grayson: *Argh my cousin pinned me down tickled me I was laughing loud bloody hell.*

Markus: *Hahahha that's cute.*

Grayson: *Omg I nearly peed haha.*

Markus: *I was gunna ask that. I was like, What if he did.*

Grayson: *Hahah I was stop stop and swore and yelled and She stopped haha.*

Markus: *That's like tickle rape.*

Grayson: *Yep.*

Markus: *She's funny haha.*

Grayson: *yah man.*

Markus: *Wanna chat I'm soooo bored.*

Grayson: *Im guuna go mowing the lawns.*

Markus: *Aw that's okay.*

Grayson: *Sorry will do when I finish.*

To fill in the time while he's waiting, Markus walks down the hallway and removes his shirt. The warm cotton catches on his ears. He tugs and the garment comes away. He switches on the radio in the bathroom. He looks at his so-called mouse-brown ear-length hair in the narrow mirror. I like it like that, Elmyra had said. He begins shaving. Foaming. Slicing through the layer. Silence slips away from him like the cream he shaves from his skin, and a turbulent roar swashes inside his head.

Grayson's been here a kazillion times before and it has felt homely; this morning, his presence had felt like that of an old guest meeting someone new. When Gray had showered this morning, the water had rushed like riptides inside the house's copper veins. Markus'd listened to Grayson's showering at the pool's change room, mistaking, or not, the water's slapping on the concrete floor in the stall beside him for Grayson jacking his junk.

Markus swishes the last of the white shaving foam into the basin, washes the residue from his chin and cheeks and neck. He looks into the mirror at his face, chest, shoulders, biceps. Markus's ribcage could burst outward with all the things he could've ever said to Grayson and never has. Near-combustion, near-expulsion, and frustration swell in his chest. He's frightened that he'll take the razor and shear into the spaces between his ribs to release its pressure. Markus drops it into the bottom drawer of the vanity, right at the back, behind disused deodorants and aftershaves. He's looking back into the eyes looking out at him from inside the mirror.

Markus is angry with Grayson: for leaving him, for not saying what he wanted to hear. He's angry with Buff for not knowing what he's talking about. He's not quite angry, rather somewhat irritated, with the guilt Elmyra provokes in him for choosing Grayson over her. And angry with himself for choosing Grayson over everyone. No. He's angry with Grayson for being fucken oblivious. Markus undresses and contemplates his junk hanging limp between his legs. Pubes spread, a thinning bush over his stomach and down the inside of his thighs. He imagines he's someone else inside. This is not his mind. This is not his want. If it's his body on the outside and within it's not his body, it makes it easier to touch, to love. If it's someone else on the inside. If his mind becomes someone else's mind. And anyway, the heat calls for this release. The rain won't come. Each encounter has pushed to this. The man's tickle on his groin, flesh-on-flesh, blood swell. To close his eyes and go back to when the axe bit the ironbark, to when the grass was an electric brush, when Fish broke surface tension, when rough palms shook and mice shook.

He begins with a naked man wearing orange undies. Goes on with this, pretends it's wrong with self-loathing, etc. *Too late now, I'm close.* Goes on with the man, strips him naked and begins making love with him on a Sunday on the floor beside the open window. The amber curtains snap, and he smells marigolds, sweet sweat, fresh cut grass, and musk. Autumn, and the man's hand touching, the man holding him down, laughing into his chest, and the man's heavy, husky, warm breathing on … He spoons him; they're in bed, are not quite sleeping, and are whispering between the words of Cold War Kids. *A little fun for my friend*, Grayson says. *What are you going to do?* Markus says. *Whatever you'll let me do.* Grayson shifts his hands over Markus's chest, down to his belly and onto his underwear. *How's that?*

Markus cums.

He showers with Lewis McKirdy. He likes Lewis. Likes the stream slashing down into his hair and on his neck and back, and Lewis's smooth voice coming in between the rushing. He can forget everything else; he's flying high and the right way up. Three minutes, he hears

Rene's voice. Three minutes an' don't let it run while ya scrubbin' y'teeth. He wants to say, *Tight-arse*. It's not about the money, though, and Markus knows it. It's hard, when he can recall days as a small child when he'd run through a garden sprinkler. Out of the shower, Markus is flying upside down once more. The mirror's misted over, and so he wipes it away, but the condensation recovers as soon as he wipes. There's no face now, which he prefers. A crash inside him, coming down, and heat pricking his body as the radio chants Cold War Kids. Back in his own room, with faded Aquaman posters tacked to walls and small pillars of poetry piled at the bed's foot, he closes the door and opens the robe. He dresses in grey jeans and a peach-toned t-shirt. Sprays Joop.

A *cht-cht chtt* sound, followed by mewing. A wail for, say, a lost love … He finds Cat in the laundry. Its paw digs the unused kitty litter. There's no shit, no piss: Cat's scraping the little white stones into a neat pile. He grabs the trembling feline, who bites the palm of his hand hard. Markus has to wrestle to get himself free. A few deep cuts on his palm draw a steady stream of blood. He goes to the kitchen and fills a cake tin with water and Dettol, soaks the sliced skin for a few moments. Stinging runs to the tips under his nails. He bandages the wound, overcompensating as he gazes into the lounge. Grayson's not there. Markus slaps the bitten palm into his hip.

Is that you, Mark? Elba rises from the couch and

comes toward him. Your hand. She takes his bitten hand and rubs the bandage.

Cat, he says.

It bit you because it's off the street.

It's not Cat's fault.

She dusts her hands, saying, Suit yourself, and then leans them on the kitchen bench across from him. Have you seen your father?

He shakes his head.

She says, You have to go up and finish off some tree. I don't know how you finish off a tree, but ... She pushes tendrils of hair from the side of her face.

Markus says, I have to go out now.

Her hand stops somewhere at the back of her head. She closes her eyes and says, Just do it. She heads back to the couch. Stop arguing and do it.

There's a swell in Markus's chest.

From inside the shed he takes up metho and a battery-operated drill. The motorbike will be lucky to get there; he knows this as he rides it up the paddock. Nothing has fixed it yet, so he doesn't expect whatever it was that Buff's done to fix it either. Markus'll have to take it to Brute's in the next week sometime. He winds through nodding heads of grass, their florets filled with muted afternoon sunshine. The thrumming motor is incongruous as it nears the tree that he, with the help of Rene, had felled this morning. The wood is fresh and scented sweet, earthy and virginal, swathed in deep bark that's impregnated with kino. The drill's cutting piece twirls into the heart, draws up sawdust. He takes the methylated poison, sunlight glistening at the edges of its plastic bottle. He fills five drill holes. Strange to kill the thing Rene's obsessed with. But Rene says, and what Rene says, goes. He straightens the bottle, recaps. He sits back beside the stump.

There're more clouds in the sky; they cast purple shadows over the vast flatness. Maybe the vapour will break, maybe it will rain upon the land, stir the dust, twist and straighten and twist like awns. He slides a piece of Wrigley's out of its foil and begins chewing the minty flesh. The taste crisps within him, freshens his perspective. He lies on his stomach. Cocks his head to the side and selects a single stem of plains grass. He's careful of the grass's yellow spikelet as he traces his thumb and forefinger down to the waxy base. Pulls. It squeaks and plucks away. He waves it in front of him, strokes the seed head over his cheek, down his jaw, onto his neck, and closes his eyes.

At a certain time this morning, sunlight had purled through drawn lace curtains to gather, sleek, on Markus's bedroom floor. Its presence had made him think of Grayson. In the extended moments before arising to Rene's call, Markus, being naked and in bed, stroked his hand down his chest and over his cock, fingering the hair on his thigh. Most mornings, as if it'll stop him, he pictures behind closed eyes a decaying animal, like a dried-out fox carcass hanging on a fence. This morning, he knew from the moment he saw the sunlight on his floor that picturing decay would be futile. His cock swelled and his foreskin retracted. The decaying-animal image failed to fill his entire mind and instead it zoomorphised into the figure of Grayson asleep in his house. While Grayson in his entirety is not a simple sexual object, there *is* a part of him that serves as an object for exploring what Markus is feeling towards him. So, with semen spurted on his belly, Markus had dropped his foot over the side of the bed and made his toes make shadows in the streaks of sun.

One eye opens. Markus says, Fuck.

I wish I could suspend this moment, place it in the heart of the grass seeds, and that the seeds would blow away to a remote part of the country. What if those seeds took root and grew and existed forever? The creation of my own world.

Halfway home the motorbike's engine sputters, conks out.

He dismounts, kicks the front wheel, which dully resounds. The handlebars try to pivot when he curses and kicks the wheel again; pivot, say, as if to get away from him. He decides to push the bike the rest of the way. Little clouds of dust rise into the air with each step. A Murray Grey moos from the paddock beside the track and knocks its thick skull against a fence post. Haze made of a thousand and more tiny insects swarm Markus's head. He sputters their tiny bodies stuck on his lips. The motorbike will be fixed. One day. He doesn't know which. He discards the bike in Rene's shed.

Elba's snoring on the couch. A repeat of the Spanish version of *Pride and Prejudice* is playing on the telly's screen; its subtitles are in English.

He moves over to her and contemplates spitting in her semi-open mouth, not because he wants to or because he dislikes her. She's okay. She's there. Her mouth is open, asking for it. Kinda. He decides not to; that it would wake her. He came back inside for one thing. He takes up the keys for her Jeep from the kitchen table.

Markus, in Elba's Jeep, flies past Rene's ute on its way back home. Nevermind. In town, he goes around to Elmyra's like he said he would. She's home. He imagines how Buff might turn and hold her around the waist, kiss her cheek like a child might. She'd squeak and giggle and say, *You'll wake Mum up*. He'd whisper onto her warm neck, *Sorry*. With gossip running amok, Markus wonders if this hearsay will actually bring Buff and Elmyra together. Not under rose bushes or beneath geraniums but in public. Maybe at the pool, getting cherry ice-creams. Markus would like to see Elmyra happy, to see her caring for someone in a different way to how she cares for her mother, or even him. He thumps the front door shut behind him as he enters, and looks back to see if the stained-glass motif's intact. In the entry of her house, as he's removing his boots, he wishes her a happy b'day.

She asks if he'd enjoyed his own birthday party last night. I lost you, she says. I was looking for you before I left.

He could tell her that he and Grayson had broken into the public pool and gone swimming. He doesn't, because the next thing she asks is if his hand, the one Cat's bit, is okay. He listens to his woollen sock as the second leather boot slides away from his foot; the sound is a quiet exhalation. He rubs the dirt that has fallen from the bottoms of his Blundstones into the carpet. There's a buzz within his toes from static electricity.

She says, Why are you *so* dressed up?

He says, For Grayson's gig at the pub.

Oh, that, she says. I saw that on Facebook.

Elmyra's giggly and says she must come to have a few drinks before her party. She asks about Buff Burrows as she leads Markus down to her bedroom. Her room is as it's always been. A four-poster bed, and, at its foot against the wall, a sassafras dresser with a tri-fold mirror that reflects bed and room. There's a rug striped with shades of grenadine spread flat against the timber floorboards. Music comes from her iPod dock. She adjusts the music's volume low. Markie. Buff, how was he?

As always, Markus says. He lies on her bed and looks to its muted floral canopy. Indecorous.

What?

He was as Buff always is. Markus sits up.

Elmyra's at her dresser with her back to him.

137

Why Buff? he says.

What do you mean?

Buff doesn't have the greatest track record of, ah, tolerance. It's pretty much his way or the highway. Markus thinks first of the things Buff's said about Youarang, and then Georges.

Elmyra says, People are complicated.

Markus sees, in the mirror, her eyes and tight lips; sees her mother, almost.

The mother he's heard more about than he's seen. He's going off what he's created. Mrs Robinson keeps to her room. Elmyra has said before that she hardly sees her dad. His truck's had more whores than cargo while tripping to and fro the continent, or so Mrs Robinson says to Elmyra after a wine or two. Her dad works with his friend Ned, and Elmyra has never seen them apart. When her dad comes home, Ned's always with him. They get drunk and whisper at strange hours. They're best friends. They make each other happy. Markus watches as Elmyra pats her skirt and runs her fingers through her fringe, leans forward and picks the spaces between her teeth with a painted fingernail. Maybe she finds him frat/paternal. After all, her father's absent and her own brother had escaped to the city as soon as he could. No one says much about him. The silence on the absent brother is self-preservation: remembering his beaten face would be too much. This truth presses on Elmyra like the pink wax she glides over her lips and the black she pencils near her eyes.

Elmyra smiles at Markus's reflections. She says, Buff says I should've been alive in the forties. She wobbles her head to the music. She pouts and puts her fingers at the base of her head, strokes her hair outward.

When their parents were close friends and went out to dinners together (before her father ran away with Ned) Elmyra and Markus would stay behind at her house. Markus'd curl up on Elmyra's bed with her mother's atlas spread before him. She'd have rented old Monroe movies. She'd sit on the end of the bed and watch them, rewinding and re-playing certain scenes over and over. He, meanwhile, would chuckle behind her as he read out from the atlas place names that sounded like body parts.

It's stupid to relive what's dead, Markus says as he lies back down on her bed again. His shoulders ease into the doona. He rubs his eyes. Anyway. You look magnificent.

She sniffs. Please.

Please what?

Marilyn was magnificent.

A goddess.

Looking for her god.

It's his turn to sniff dismissively. He says, There are no gods, only goddesses. He's lying on his stomach now, fist propping up his chin. He tilts his head, trying to see around her body.

In her reflections, her powder brush pretends it's

missed a patch of skin, compensates, overcompensates, and creates a streak of deep blush. She asks, And how d'you figure?

Goddesses are the ones that give birth.

There has to be at least a god for the -dess to fall in love with. Didn't Rene ever tell you about the birds and bees, Markie?

Don't be silly. Goddesses don't need love.

She is done with the powder brush, and she declares, Then how can there be either gods or goddesses if the two never meet? Her eyes are busy on the perfume bottles before her.

He says, You're silly, and rolls onto his back.

She sighs. My party's at eight. We can get Buff to pick us up from Grayson's gig and take us out to the farm.

Yair. He did say he'd rock up to the pub before yours.

Oh, cool. Well, that's if you want.

Yair.

And Cecily?

Markus blinks. Mm.

Will she come?

Dunno, El. But I guess so; she does cling to Grayson like a too-tight boob tube.

Elmyra laughs. I don't think so.

She sees him every day.

They *are* a couple, Markie.

I've never seen someone look so desperate to, to …

Look *what?* Elmyra's fastening a tangerine ribbon below the fringe wave of her Monroe hair. She runs the ends by her ears and ties off at the base of her head. The ribbon tails fall down her back.

He says, What does Cecily have that a million other women prefer not to show?

She says, Some people exaggerate because they don't have a clear idea of themselves, others do it to make a point.

He looks at the way she's moving her head, her hands, her lips: watching herself, fine-tuning. After a childhood spent closely together and a chaste period of 'going out' in high school, they've drifted from each other. Perhaps she has a molten core, bubbling and waiting to erupt through her surface. If she does, she's hidden it well over the years.

She clears her throat before continuing. All I hope is that Grayson appreciates the effort.

Whose effort?

Whoever puts in the most in the way he wants; he picks pieces from people and the rest, well, you can just forget about. Elmyra sprays a perfume on her neck and then replaces the glass bottle.

He isn't sure they're talking about Cecily and Grayson anymore, which is why he wants to bring Elmyra down, to say something about her dressing as Marilyn — how it's her own kind of picking, picking, forgetting — but her actions are mysterious, almost cabalistic. Except, maybe, to Cecily, which would explain Elmyra's defensiveness and the air of conspiracy, founded or not. And maybe that's a part of it, like the Monroe quote blu-tacked to Elmyra's mirror: *I am trying to find myself.*

He steers away. He says, So you weren't at the pool this morning?

Elmyra hums a reply.

Where were you? Markus suspects she was with Buff, but wants her to tell him so herself.

She's twisting the perfume bottles, turning the labels away. The light from the setting sun shines into the shapely glass bottles and onto the myriad colours inside: robin egg, lavender, pistachio, yolk.

He says, I was there with Grayson. And Cecily.

Of course.

From the bed, he imagines how Buff might undress Elmyra's body and take her silken-skinned breasts in each of his hands, how he might not draw breath until he kisses her, how the sheets might swish. He wonders: how does Grayson kiss? One thing leads to another, they say. A restless, gentle biting of lips, holding on to himself as his skin heats with rubbing and touching? He doesn't know how it works. Wonders what it would be like to have Grayson push himself into him. To hold a few moments. Grayson's body might be electric against his body, and he might have flapping excitement in his chest and stomach, and trembling in his arms, legs, and a thudding in his chest. He might understand himself. The anger might subside. He might be at peace. Wonders if this, too, is what Buff seeks in Elmyra, and even in Markus when he'd asked, Have y'ever? Wondering brings Markus no closer to understanding. It brings him no closer than acting out his imaginings might. He rubs his palm over his mouth.

Elmyra says, Was the water divine?

We were only there for a little bit.

Oh?

Yair, he says, Grayson had to leave to start getting ready for his gig.

I see.

He ended up going home and sleeping. Markus laughs.

Elmyra turns around. Are you sure your hand is okay?

What? He looks at the bandage, can't explain. He remembers Cat's teeth slicing through his flesh.

You ready? she asks.

There's a while before the gig.

So? She steps up and takes his hand.

He mouths, La di da.

Everything's forgotten when she spins him around. He bends to increase the volume of her music, a 40s song. Shirley Thoms, she says as if he's meant to know. They dance. She sings. From the far end of the hallway they must look very grown-up. He holds her shoulders, and she holds his waist. He's sure they're doing it wrong.

The music yodels, which catches Markus off-guard. He doesn't want to laugh; doesn't feel it would be okay. So he concentrates on Elmyra's skin. There's a smooth line from her chin to her neck, and to where her flesh disappears under her salmon-pink shirt. As they dance, he looks at a brown mole visible beneath her collar.

Markie. She laughs a little. My mum's home. She spins away and lowers the music. We'll disturb her.

That shouldn't stop us.

What's that mean?

I don't know. He suppresses a growl and is astounded he felt like he needed to growl. We should go. Help Grayson set up. He moves backward and wipes his bandaged hand over his chest.

Markie?

He hates her calling him that. Hates everybody — Rene, Elba, Buff, Cecily — calling him anything other than Markus.

My name is Markus. My name is Markus. My name is Markus.

Markie, are you okay?

Her window looks out into the flat landscape. The sun dipping behind the cliff tops. The sky deepens in blue and more clouds are moving overhead. A flock of cockatoos float across the plain, coming in to roost. The Depression is quite creative in its ways of manifesting harshness; although, looking upon this scene, you wouldn't guess so.

What're you thinking? he asks.

She shrugs.

She asks what he's thinking.

He hesitates. The cliffs, he says. It's almost like the horizon's been moved in closer and raised up higher.

Almost is most, she says.

Then I'm sure Narioka's the end of the earth.

She smiles at him and picks up her bag. She suggests they go now if they want to make her party afterward.

He says he needs a piss. In her bathroom, he locks the door behind him.

What an odd thing for her to say. *Almost is most.* He has the second-last piece of Wrigley's gum. Its mint flavour calms.

He cups water from the tap, wets his face, streaks his hair back with the leftover, and it stands in tufts around his ears. A mane. He sniffs his underarms to check if they're still good. The mustard light in here is nauseating, and distracts. The sooner he gets to Grayson's gig, the better. He checks his mobile. No messages. Nothing. The cunt said he'd ring. He sits on the dunny's lid. The least Gray could do is send a smiley back to Markus's last text. Markus jigs his legs. He steps across to the basin again. Fuck.

Elmyra makes him nervous, but even that word's too loose. Her eyes are the problem, let alone what she says — what have we actually been talking about? Whatever. Her eyes: like she sees into his imagination. Can she see the version of Grayson that inhabits Markus? Fuck no. He hopes no.

He gulps water and wets his hands again. Droplets glisten and plummet from his lips. He rubs his fingers over his eyes, cheeks, and drags their pads toward his neck. Slippy skin. He runs his palms through his hair again; the mane remains untamed.

In year seven or eight, he used to poke a compass into his legs in an attempt to centre himself. Now he has this: Grayson's gig. It has meaning. It gives him purpose. Not like his mind and its orange-underweared man — but he can't help its currents, and he can't slow or change its directions. Grayson had once observed that people force themselves on Markus, urging him to do what he doesn't want to do. Like Buff wanting Markus to man up. And Elmyra wanting him to be, do. And Grayson. What is he? Markus will not be what they want him to be. He decides that he can't stay here in the Depression and its endless paddocks. He puts his fingers on the mirror. Their tips run down beside his reflection. *Some people exaggerate because they don't have a clear idea of themselves, others do it to make a point.*

The pub's red bricks are old enough that some parts have begun to decay and, with the tin-roofed veranda running along its façade, the front, from a distance, looks more like an old man watching over his flock with his cap drawn low than a hub of the community. By the time Markus and Elmyra arrive, the sky's spitting rain. Cool wind blows rain beads about as if snowflakes. Markus leans against a veranda post, whose white paint's flaky and crumbles on his clothes. The white flakes fall to the ground. The windows behind him, which have tacky orange blinds drawn over their insides, give off apricot light. Two long trapeziums of it stretch right out to the angle car-parks lining the front of the pub. He can't see if this light reaches the road. He lets rain swirl into his eyes. His hair must look as it had earlier today, when he'd risen from the swimming pool. He watches Cecily get out of a car that has pulled up, and, from the passenger side, Grayson. They're dressed neatly. Cecily slams her door. When she steps away from the vehicle, the point of her shoe catches on the bitumen. Her trip sounds like a loud slap across the face. Grayson raises his head, lowers it. She reclaims her composure and her heels are resplendent in the empty street. Grayson stands with the top half of his body bent inside the car's boot. Markus can see him outlined by the light from inside the car. Cecily holds her handbag aloft her head so her hair doesn't get wet. Markus can't bring himself to call it proper rain, like good-for-a-crop rain, even though it's making things damp. (Not that he knows what a good-for-a-crop rain looks like in terms of its goodness for crops.) He's becoming less aware of Elmyra beside him. Her weight shifting from leg to leg.

The pub's carpet is worn. Beside the entry and opposite the bar, a wood fire heats the low-ceilinged room. A group of older men, including Brute Burrows, stand around it. Markus nods at Brute and wonders why Buff isn't with him.

A short while later, halfway through a lemonade (or something stronger), Grayson comes over from setting up and kisses Elmyra on the cheek. You scrub up well, he says. Make this champ look half decent. He hugs Markus and pats his back. Says, Sorry I was a bit stiff before. Grayson's voice vibrates on Markus's chest as they hug.

By the end of their pots, the pub's patronage has grown. There's incomprehensible chatter and occasional bursts of laughter.

You coming to my party? Elmyra's got her bag over her shoulder. She sits on the bar stool as if it's not good enough for her arse. She could almost be squatting over it.

El, please, says Markus.

Grayson says, When is it?

Tonight. Eight.

Markus skols. Says, Grayson's not played yet.

Time waits for no man, she says.

Grayson buys them another beer. Markus tries to say, No thanks, but Gray forces the pot into his hand. #YOLO. He lifts the glass, lets his legs fall butchly astride like the other men in here, and sips. He's uncomfortable and spotlighted. Alcohol will ease him. Every real man's at perpetual ease, their smiles ready for the next dirty joke. He's not quite smiling yet, too anxious about the little barneys breaking out in patterns across the room. Better to quell them with bitter lager, for isn't that why you come here — to get away from the blues at home and to drown the ones you meet? Grayson still hasn't started playing. And at the end of their second or third beer, Elmyra pokes her nose into Markus's hair near his ear.

She asks, Where's Buff?

Markus, raising the pot ready for another swig, says, Buff said he was coming.

Grayson nods his beer at her and says, Never trust a man who gives a nickname the first time you meet him, fucken unreliable.

Elmyra fans her face with a stubby holder. Lots of things are, Gray.

You wouldn't be talkin' about Markus here?

Fuck off the both of you, Markus says. He goes to buy the next round.

Slumping in the mucky corner is old man McGregor with a yellow beard and yellow fingernails. He says, Been carting hay to the cattle this arvo; the weather forecast has me shakin' like a dog shittin' razor blades, so the pub's as good a place as any to pass out. Maybe never wake, ay, he chuckles. His eyelids are red and weep at the corners.

Can't even see the colour of his eyes that squeeze with every word more than a syllable.

Markus pays and edges away. Down the bar a bit, he gives Grayson, who's holding Cecily around her waist, the pot of beer. Elmyra and Cecily chatter. Grayson's fingers press harder into Cecily's hip's flesh. And at seeing this, Markus says, I need a piss.

The toilet door wheezes closed. The sickly-sweet ammonium stench of urinal blocks floats through the bathroom.

Better make room for more. Grayson's followed him in. Bloody expensive piss. He mentions staying at Markus's place after Elmyra's party. Ren won't mind me a second night, ay?

So long as you don't chuck everywhere. Markus laughs. He says, I wasn't planning on going.

Yair way.

No way.

Yair. Way. Then Grayson says, Elmyra'll be shitty if you don't.

They re-zip their flies.

Markiss. Grayson grabs him by the shoulders. Goin' t'her party doesn't mean ya stickin' with her. He leans in and muckily presses his mouth against Markus's forehead.

Markus says, I'll drive — you're fucken half-in-the-bag.

Back in the bar, he and Grayson get a fourth (or fifth) beer before going to stand with Cecily and Elmyra.

You two took your time, says Cecily. She winks.

Markus feels a tug on his sleeve. Pulls away and it pulls back. His head swipes around and Elmyra, looking near the door, says she has to leave. He scrunches an eye at her and says, The fuck y'on about? His tongue liberated by booze. *He* doesn't need to leave. He drinks. He's anticipating how the plucking notes, which Grayson has not begun playing, will enchant him. He'll stay in this spot. He has a slight smile now.

Elmyra pushes past all the hard-bitten maleness in order to leave through the frosted-glass door.

Markus — making out like it's his duty, but in fact, feeling guilt-ridden — quaffs the pot and picks a sweating spring roll from a plastic plate along the bar. He makes his way outside, feeding his face.

Wind blows Elmyra's hair out of place as she stands by a bollard, tapping the screen of her mobile. One of the elongated trapeziums of apricot-coloured light from the pub's window surrounds her.

It's becoming colder with this storm. The moon lights clouds that're yet to combine, and there're twigs being stripped from the trees. He looks at the car park. The bollards mark a skinny path between this and the front of the pub. He lifts up a straight-ish twig, walks to Elmyra and pokes into her arm.

What're you doin'?

Going to my party, she says.

He's self-satisfied and whatnot, taller than the trees, taller than the clouds when rain falls. He taps the twig against a bollard next to hers. Phallic. He says, Who're you texting?

She's quiet.

He spots a small hole, under the size of a ten-cent piece, dug into the crumbling bitumen. He pokes the twig down, swivels and pulls back out. Attached to the end, with its mouthparts crushed, is a bardi grub.

Elmyra says, That's fucken disgusting.

He says, You should eat it. You've had nothing. And offers the larva to her.

You should; it's what you deserve, she says.

The sky's chilled beads land on his cheeks; they're falling harder. He tells her he had an hors-d'œurve.

They're spring rolls, Markie, and you've killed that … thing, for no reason.

It was going to kill the tree. He uses the stick to point a tree out nearby.

They don't do that, she says.

He might, never know with a wood-eater, he'll chew right through the core.

I don't have time for this.

He flicks the grub away. The twig follows.

She informs him that Buff's coming to get her. Wind blows her hair wild. He's taking me to my party. The one I set up.

Markus says, I'm waiting for Grayson.

You'll always be waiting for him.

Moments before, he'd felt taller than trees and clouds. With a simple statement, he's felled and sodden.

Lightning flashes. Or a streetlight's globe blew.

She says, If he comes before … She looks up into his face before she turns to look into the darkness.

Stop pretendin' like we're everyone else, El. A swell in his chest and a salty burn in his eyes, either for the truth she spat or because he resents her as much as he depends on her.

She moves away from him. Light dapples her body. The wind blows the hem of her skirt and, looking down the road for distant headlights, she pats the material against her skin.

Dust, it must've been dust blowing into his eyes. Oh, we forgot ya present, he says. We'll be late to ya partay. He turns and spits into the wirilda (*Acacia retinodes*) growing near the pub's door.

Thunder.

Inside, Markus scans the floor for Grayson and sees him near the fireplace, smiling as he checks Brute Burrows on the chin. Markus hurries over.

Brute sniggers, the fat about his neck wobbles like a proud cock's wattles, and he says, Do that ahgen, mate. Brute sits his half-sunk pot on the fireplace opposite the bar, straightens his body and becomes elephantine.

The other boozers, with dirty unshaven faces, exchange eye-jabs.

Markus is sweaty-palmed. How the fuck did this happen?

Some of the elders laugh or breathe heavier with nervousness, passing this teeny confrontation off as light-heartedness. Juss a blue b'tween mates.

No harm, ay. No harm done, says Grayson.

Behind, the bartender cuffs a pot on the wooden bar top.

Grayson turns.

The bartender nods and crosses his arms and says, Youse fellas get ya shit together or get out.

Tell this shithead to fucken piss orf, says Brute, stepping a little forward and yelling to be heard.

Grayson laughs; short like ha ha and inflected on the end, posing a profound question.

Brute blocks the light from the doorway between the bar and dining room. He raises his hands and his body seems to speak. His body tells the tale of the country he's from. *I come from a country where Ned Kelly's king. I'll king-hit this li'l' derro — nah! King-hit's a coward punch. King Coward. No. Two, maybe three or more punches on the chin. I'll be the talk of the town if I bring this larrikin down.*

Markus acts. He pushes Brute, follows him into the dining room. Move. Move fast, take the cunt by surprise. Move. Move fast because Grayson might be hurt. Brute grunts.

On ya toes, someone shouts.

Markus takes Brute by the collar, jumper-punches him, and his heaviness aches in Markus's knuckles. He swings the weight around. Pushes Brute back toward the wall beside the door. Huffs.

Righto fellas, stop ya rot, the bartender yells.

In the dining room, Markus steers Brute again at the wall so his back cracks against it. Pulls him away, pulling a stubborn anchor. Spittle from both their mouths. Brute bends a little, the fat on his stomach stops him from going double-over. Move. Move. Taking his strength to heave this rock, Markus pushes it forward. Lets go. Brute's head arches, conks on the brickwork — Fucken 'ell, he pants. The elder men gather at the door, none enter. And surely, beyond the barricade of age, the young lads dance regardless.

The bartender throws Markus out. He stumbles into the night, which is pouring with rain. Elmyra is gone. Markus drives Cecily back to her house because she says she's too crook to go to El's. After they drop Cecily off, Grayson says, She's not sick. We had a fight before gettin' to the pub.

What's that? Markus is driving the short distance to Gray's place.

She's at me to leave IGA — she says it's not proper work — an' she's at me to give up giggin' to get some bullshit apprenticeship.

The car pulls up in the drive. Markus says, You need to do what's best for you.

Grayson hums. I just need to forget it for the moment, he says, there's always tomorrow.

It's raining harder, and the boys dash through the front yard and around the back of the house. Grayson stretches up to the rafters of the back patio and pulls down a key to the back door. He replaces the key in the rafters and heads inside. He opens a bottle of vodka in the kitchen. It's semi-dark and cold, and Grayson's smiling as he reads the vodka's label. Espresso — eee-yuck. Can ya pour this? He hands the bottle to Markus and then wanders into the lounge.

Mixer? Markus pours a standard measure and a little bit over into two glasses.

See what's in the fridge.

Where's your mum?

Not here, Grayson replies.

When's she back? Markus decides on Coke Zero. He tops the glasses. Hazy eyed, he's glad this place has the same layout as his.

Grayson's bending to the fireplace in the lounge and fiddling with a match. He drops it. Don't break li'l' guy, he says. The match head ignites and lights the kindling fire. Closing its door, he asks if they're heading out to Elmyra's.

I guess, says Markus as he sits on the couch. He feels guilty. He hands the second drink to his mate, who sits beside him.

Fark, Grayson says after a sip. How much vodka d'ya put?

Markus says he needs it.

Grayson sips. S'alright, he says. I forgive ya.

For what? Markus laughs.

For being you.

Markus coughs. There's been one other time that Grayson said he forgave Markus — for being you. Though the first time, he'd phrased it differently. It's just you. On that camping trip, year eight or nine, the night Buff had stayed and said he was texting some girl. Buff said, Shit my rufus is hard. Idiot. Anyway, Gray had laughed and asked a question Markus hadn't heard. It was then that Buff turned to Markus and asked, You listenin'? Yes. Yes, because Markus knew the bastard was texting Elmyra — always had been. What of it? Buff scoffed. Nothing, just don't fuck her over. And there was a pause before Buff said, I reckon there'll be some fucking. He laughed. Grayson laughed. Markus had waited until they'd finished and said, You're both feral pigs.

You've said that once before, Markus says. Remember? Nah, cunt.

When we went camping and Buff came along. And you said, *carn, Markus, it's just you*. It's just nothing. It's not me.

I didn't mean it as a bad thing. Grayson sips the drink; his face scrunches as he swallows. He says, It *is* just you. He puts his glass down on the coffee table, springs up and goes to his bedroom, quick-shuffling down the hall and yelling, Gotta charge me phone.

The night is fragmented, and Markus wants to say, *Slow down so I can follow*. He wants to stay stretching across the couch and talking shit with Gray till they both pass out. Instead, he pours Grayson's vodka down the kitchen sink. They've both had enough. The fridge door has a few pictures on it. One is held up with a magnet from the Big Strawberry. It's of two boys: the first, Grayson, lays belly-down on a skateboard, his arms stretched out in front, and the second, Markus, lays legs-forward on his back on top of Gray. They're smiling and their hair's captured in a perpetual wave. They must've come down the skate ramp.

The photo peeks out from under a calendar. Grayson's mother's schedule scrawled in tiny handwriting, smudged in places, to fit it all in. AM shift, PM shift, PM, PM, AM, AM, AM, PM, written on the days of the week. AM highlighted in yellow with a smiling sun beside it and PM highlighted in blue with a crescent moon beside it. There're hair appointments wedged between the days, too, as well as when pay is expected, and Grayson's shifts at the supermarket, his gigs at the pubs, his own hair appointments, a dental appointment. One Sunday, at the end of this month, the words *Mum & son day?* are pencilled in.

Markus heads down the hallway.

Grayson's on his bed with his smartphone over his

face, humming a melody.

You didn't get to play your gig, says Markus.

Grayson laughs. Fuckers don't deserve it.

What about your gear?

Ay?

Guitar an' that.

Gray shrugs. Get it tomorrow.

Markus shivers again, like that saying someone's walked over his grave, and says, Can I borrow a jumper?

Grayson rolls off the bed. What d'ya say? He bends forward and puckers his lips.

Fuck off. Markus opens the wardrobe door and takes out a hoodie.

Grayson walks around the bed. Look here, he says at the condensation on the bedroom window. Started earlier an' that's why I was late to the pub an' that somehow started Cecily off ... I just wanted t' watch it. Must be cause of how cold it is. Global warmin' an' crazy weather. He's talking as if a child dreaming. Can you even think what it'll be like in fifty years?

We'll probably all be dead, Gray.

Why's that?

No bees left in Narioka.

So?

Rene says it's right for small producers to hand-pollinate, but what about those massive wheat runs in New South?

We'll all starve.

Plus the drought and no jobs.

An' them extremists.

Markus sniffs. World's fucked.

Grayson has, the whole conversation, kept his eyes on the condensation forming on the window. The lamplight casts moody shadows around him.

Yes. He is magnificent.

What can we do, but?

Markus tries to form a reply, but can only shrug.

Grayson starts to write in the condensation. His shirtless torso stretches across the corner of the mattress, his jean's fly undone. He mutters. It's quiet enough to be cryptic. He takes his finger away. His nail's chewed back almost to a painful shortness. With the pad of his finger, he's written in the water *perder nuestras mentes* and underneath *mi compañeros*.

I don't know what that means. Markus draws a cock and balls beneath it.

Grayson dons a new shirt and jumper. My colour? He spins and falls back on the bed. We could stay, he says. The fire's blazin'.

Markus can't say anything. It's billowing inside and too big to fit out his mouth.

It's raining. Grayson closes his eyes, rests his palms over

the material covering his belly. He looks asleep. He breathes out a word, Elmyra. He stands up and roughs his hair, looking at his reflection in the glass of a picture frame.

Fuck me dead, says Markus as he jitters the gear stick.

They've taken Elba's Jeep. It's struggling in the cold, the storm.

Pick a gear an' she'll go. Grayson lifts Markus's hand away and with his own shifts the stick into place. The Jeep resumes. Music full. The vodka's awoken Grayson, where the beer had dulled him. He beats.

Markus begins driving, a tingle in his hands and a blur in his eyes. Vodka's had the opposite effect on him. It's vanquished him, and he's numb under its influence. He attaches his sight on Grayson.

It happens quick.

The fuck y'doin? Markus yells.

Grayson casts away the efforts to stop him. He's climbing out the passenger window. He's sitting very far forward on the window's ledge.

The steering wheel wobbles, the car follows.

Markus ducks down near the gears and can see Gray's face outside through the windscreen. Markus hears himself yell, Get the fuck in.

The road speeds and the accelerator drops further to the floor. With his head and torso hanging outside the vehicle, Grayson closes his eyes. Doesn't hear. Raindrops gather on his face. Slippy skin.

Back.

Grayson doesn't register.

Come back.

The vehicle moves on to the wrong side of the road. Sways back to the left. Speed because fear. Trying to fix this makes Markus afraid. Grayson yells, valiant as a screeching cockatoo, his voice velvet and rounded in the night. Upward to the stars he calls, hunting or chasing them down. The car moves further left onto the brittle gravel edge. Sways back to the centre of the bitumen. Markus reaches out, touches Gray's legs inside the car. Grayson wobbles. His eyes flick open. He latches onto the Jesus bar. Smiles and pushes Markus's hand away with a clumsy foot. Markus hears the rushing tyres. The car slides and its side takes out several guide posts. *Bang. Bang. Bang. Bang. Bang.* Dips into the table drain. Rolls. Slides. Screeches. Rolls another half. Lurches. And lands upturned on its dented, buckled roof. The headlights flicker on a paddock of yellow grass.

III.

The flood

We were born toward the end of last century, so we saw the Lake the one time it filled, which was several years back. At the same time it froze, and then broke up and overflowed. An 'ephemeral lake' — also seasonal, intermittent, episodic, temporary — is a watercourse that doesn't have water flow for the entire year or for many years. Some might flow for more than six months each year while others flow every six years, sixty years, etc. Water sources for ephemeral lakes can be groundwater or surface run-off. Agricultural developments and construction work can alter the water flow and cause an ephemeral system's flow to be disturbed, declined, or even disrupt its very ephemerality. When the Lake filled, it filled from excess groundwater captured on the Plain. The Plain's unwanted water was released from the otherwise overregulated system up there, flowed toward the lip of the cliffs and poured down into the Depression, filling the Lake and the tributary creek that cuts through the middle of Narioka.

Narioka's nickname, Noaks, first appeared to my ears during high school. Someone said, There's not a lot of opportunity in Noaks for the young.

I'd often stare at my naked body in the mirror, thinking of this statement and thinking about the hair coming out like shag carpet in my armpits and crotch, thinning over my chest and showing itself on my legs, on my arse. This puberty thing is misshapen for such a long time. In the shower, on any given morning, I shampoo my pubes and become hard. I shoot my load at the tiled wall and wash the silky white cum away.

The school bus picks me up from out the front of an old church. The building itself is no larger than a standard bedroom, which is why the townspeople way back when decided to disuse it and build five more in the township of Narioka, all under different denominations. This old church waits for a Catholic congregation. Wispy strands of native grasses grow nestled against its cream-coloured render, which has crumbled away in some places. For a church, you'd expect to see a steeple and a stained-glass window; this building has neither. I'm thankful for it, because at least its inset doorway provides shelter when it's raining. Some mornings on the bus into school, and when the rain is falling, I watch the rainfall patter against the glass pane and trickle down. The droplets become sperm gametes — semen, spoof, sprog, spunk, splooge, scum, seed. Become the cream of some young guy careening to somewhere out of sight. One droplet pauses and through it, I see the landscape made miniature, as if inside a crystal ball. Your bluish shadow grows more vibrant as you run up your drive to the bus's door. But there is no you this morning. The bus rocks onward past your place without even slowing.

I sink into the leather seat and hide my eyes from the glare off the side of the road; the corrugation rattles the vehicle and, in turn, shifts my junk. The head of my cock starts brushing against the cotton of my underwear. Boner. Bummer.

Fuck you, puberty.

I put my bag on my lap before I get up, and one of the Drumanure boys across from me says, You got a stiffy?

I say, Nah, I'm getting this. And pull the rotting sandwich from my bag and piff it at him.

When I break free from the stuffy interior of the bus, I wander across the bus shelter to the dusty oval beside. It has yellow-brown clumps of grass. Those boys pass a faded red leather Sherrin to-and-fro, thudding it with their heavy feet through the chipped white goal posts. Under the sky, the boys are dampened gold as the grass itself, yet unlike the grass, the boys are vivid, moving, and alive. Ancient predators that toss and wrestle and watch for the opposition. Even on a winter morning such as this, their bodies are gently grunting and pretty.

Teacher says, Be careful, because as first aid officer I don't want to have to give someone CPR and call ahead for an ambulance. What terrible news to deliver to a mother.

Watching the boys' bodies, I have to turn away. I meet up with Elmyra on the sideline. I lay down on my back, on the damp grass, with my knees bent, feet on the ground. I breathe in the cool morning air deep, moisture underneath, and look up into the infinite sky-blue space. I cover my eyes. The thudding football and the chorusing chants of footy lingo, strangely religious, tumble into my mind. I breathe out.

What are you thinking? Elmyra says. She's sitting on her folded-up waterproof parker.

I want to tell her little stories of my internal made-up world. The words are bigger than my throat and can't escape. She'll only hear the faintness, with no trace of meaning.

Nothing.

Why don't you play?

I couldn't.

It's just a game. It's not serious.

I repeat myself.

Go on. She sits up.

El, no. I don't like the game.

She pushes my side, as if trying to roll me over. I swipe her hand away, sit up, stand, and walk back through the school buildings.

Terracotta-coloured foliage crumples in the corners of the locker bay; light ambers intensified by the sunlight contrasting against the blue paint of the lockers. Compulsory chip wrappers — pink and green — twist themselves in, as do fewer Ducat's OJ bottles, drunk dry at lunchtime yesterday. The rows are each three individual lockers high — totally un-American, even though the young adults who occupy them speak American idiom, idly and ignorantly. You and I included. Mine's a middle locker at the end of the row, where the main pathways into the school buildings intersect. I have no other reason to have come here than to escape from Elmyra, from the football players. I brush some crumbs, with a single index finger, from the inside of my locker; they are like grains of sand dislocated from a distant shore. I thump the locker door shut and shackle it with a brass padlock.

More buses return from the farmlands and pull up on the bus road, which runs beside the football oval. Georges will be on one of them, drawn out from his family's cherry orchard. He'll be coming into the bay soon.

First, you.

I say, You weren't on the bus this morning?

Nah, you say, I got a ride in with me ma.

You've been in town for a few years, moved from some other part of the countryside. Your presence is a lifetime; the first time I laid eyes on you was as if I was seeing a lost friend returned. We'd met at a drought fundraiser in the skate park; your mother took a picture of us sharing a skateboard down a ramp. The drought lasted a few more years and then the people in the city declared it 'broken'. The drought never broke here.

I hadn't seen you coming across the courtyard because the thick fog is bearing down as low as it can get, so you gathered quickly into a whole at the corner of my vision. I hear familiar music flicker my attention. In the misty-grey, your iPod plays a Cold War Kids song, 'Out Of The Wilderness'.

Your locker is above mine. I step aside. Pretending the Cold War Kids is what we first found in common is easier for me than to put words to what it is that keeps me attached to you. I say, They're having a concert in the city.

A gig, yair.

On the 21st.

I was gunna say the 19th.

Dew on the edge of the veranda has frozen as it has come to drip. Underneath these frozen drips, Georges walks into the bay. His locker is beneath mine, so we step aside to allow him to kick his bag into the locker. Georges has been working on a spacer in his left ear. For the last six weeks, he's had three tapered plugs that, incrementally, have grown the hole in his lobe to a certain width. It's such a mechanical process.

I say, How big's the spacer now?

The piercist said six. I had to stretch the lobe again to get this in. Eight, I reckon. If I face the right way the wind whistles through like standing on a cliff top, he says. He keeps his voice nearly exclusive to his mouth, and I have to strain to hear him. The tunnel's made of stainless steel and, though hollow, the front has a small marine symbol: an anchor.

This is when you step onto the garden-bed curb beside him and say, Hmm, not for me.

It's a form of self-harm, says Georges with a smirk.

Pretty clichéd compared to others, I say.

You reach out and touch the tunnel.

Georges's head leans into that touch.

You let go of the spacer.

I watch you fiddle with a piece of chewing gum — your solid finger sliding around as you try easing a piece from the new Wrigley's wrap. You slip off the curb as you place the gum between your teeth. Your foot falls into some mud in the gutter.

Before we have to go to homeroom, we leave the locker bay and head around to the Art Wing veranda: a once-polished-but-now-faded scuffed stretch of decking about a half-metre off the ground. Apparently, raising a building up on stilts helps to keep it cool, but the most use we have for that space underneath is sliding our empty chip packets between the slats when we can't be arsed going to the bin. We sit on the Art Wing — morning, recess, and at lunch — because it's near a line of liquidambar (*styraciflua*) and close to where our homeroom is, but, between us, I think it's more to do with it being further away from where Teacher wanders on a routine yard-duty round. We sit to one end near the bubbler taps and, on the other side of them, the boys' toilets.

This morning we sit on the edge of the veranda, and you light up a cigarette; the fog is enough to cover your illicit action.

You boys going to the show? Georges says. He takes a puff on your cigarette.

You shrug.

I say, Probably not. And refuse a drag on the cigarette.

Shame, says Georges.

Conscious of the smell, I say, I don't wanna get caught in homeroom.

Georges laughs. Says, You take things so literally.

I don't know what he means, so, like a child, I slide back on the deck to where the wood meets the brick wall.

You continue smoking at the edge of the veranda, looking out into the fog to god knows what.

Georges says over his shoulder, I meant shame about not going to the show. He exhales a lungful of smoke as he slides back to the wall, too. He rests his head against the bricks and closes his eyes.

The boys' toilet door breaks open and, like a flock of squawking cockatoos, several boys burst out — some run past us along the Art Wing, another jumps past you, scruffing up your hair as he does. They disappear into the fog. One of the last boys out of the loo comes cackling, sliding out the door. He looks at Georges sitting beside me. He finds his feet and skips over. He puts his feet either side of Georges's tranquil body and, turning to me to give me the gnarly sign, he pumps his junk into Georges's face. After a few quick jabs, he dashes off to rejoin his mates.

Georges's eyes remain closed, perhaps a little tighter. I have some paintings going in the show, he says.

I think I should ask him if he's okay, but I don't. The boy that did it to him is captain of the first eighteen, and I, captain of the thirds.

First class of the day after homeroom: geography. For a teacher who teaches everything we should have a special nickname. A clever nickname. We call the teacher, simply, Teacher. You are sitting beside me, singing. We two, along with the eighteen other students, have our writing books out — my 96 pages, your 128 — and hand-me-down Jacaranda atlases. The sun's midway through the morning sky, the classroom too cool.

Over the cliffs is the Plain — an expanse of swaying grass. Teacher moves a finger on the wall map from the dot indicating Narioka, over the hachured contour line indicating the escarpment, and stops somewhere out on the Plain. Here is nothingness. Then, moving a finger back to and circling around Narioka, Teacher says, Here, everything. But, Teacher says, it's not quite certain how the Depression was created. We know the Depression is over a million years old. And, prior to Europeans, was occupied by an Indigenous nation. Being river people, fishing occupied most of their time, and a rich network of rivers, lagoons, creeks, and wetlands kept them strong and healthy with fish and wildlife. Water is now so regulated, though, as an irrigation system upstream that the natural waterways have become ephemeral: they only run if the authorities let water down or there's excess surface run-off. Despite this, the Narioka township was founded inside the Depression and on the edge of the creek running out of the Lake. And, subsequently, within the first generation of European arrival, the Indigenous population of this area was reduced by eighty-five per cent. Teacher's hands rub together, preparing their gestures for an announcement.

But I choose to look out the window as Teacher dictates the task for the lesson. A tickle at my elbow. You, looking straight ahead with fake attention, have slid a torn piece of paper toward me. I unfold it. It has your mobile number. When Elmyra first got a phone, she thrust the device at me and said, What're your deets? I pull out my phone and add your number.

After class, we dump our books in our lockers and head for the tuck shop. Elmyra waves us down. She's at the table in the corner, in front of the caged wall-heater. You push past the humans, all at various stages of pubescence. Chairs screak on the lino, and the wall clock falls to the floor. Nobody picks it up, even though the tuck shop lady yells, I won't know the bloody time. Elmyra's tapping on the lit screen of her smartphone.

When she looks up, I can see movement behind her irises. Perhaps it's the hearsay: her father ran away with his best mate last Tuesday. Elmyra's nails are clear and shiny, diamond-like, except at their tips, where the nails overhang her fingers by a millimetre or two. Their tips are painted pastel-orange. In her sky-blue cotton dress, her tanned skin looks deeper. She's altered her uniform: scooped out the décolletage, heightened the waist. Her eye make-up is faultless: pointed and neat. She's Marilyn today, and, as always, her hair is done likewise. She's beautiful, and perhaps I'm in love with her.

I turn away to see that you're looking at me oddly. What you say — i.e., Do you want a sausage roll in a roll — doesn't match your expression.

You meet Cecily in the line at the counter, kissing her on the neck. You've been going out for a few months, and last week told me you two 'did it'. I asked what it was like and you fobbed me off with a laugh, followed by quickly licking your top lip.

We eat lunch and then have PE class. Georges skips ahead of us, and when we get inside the change room, he slinks into a cubicle away from the communal changing area.

One of the boys says, He needs to hide his boner.

Another boy says, Go and suck 'im off, gesturing with his hand in front of his mouth.

Nah, the first boy says, did him this morning — wasn't worth the pain.

The second boys scoffs, You wouldn't be the one in pain, mate. He winks on the sly.

The entire change room seems to laugh.

And I turn my back on them to quietly change into my PE kit. Left out, distant like an island afloat at sea.

You ask if I'm okay.

Why wouldn't I be?

All you do is shrug; I could rip your shoulders from you. When the class is assembled out on the oval where Teacher takes us, I try to kick the footy into the afterlife.

After school, Rene's waiting in his beat-up ute beside the old derelict church. Because it's winter, the sun's dipped below the edge of the cliffs to make the Depression murky and shaded, as if a grand-scale Caravaggio. There's a tree beside the church. It must've been ring-barked some time ago, for the limbs are bare and greyish. Through the empty canopy, the sky, way up overhead and beyond, is greeny-yellow.

This is unusual: Rene waiting by the church. Someone's died, I'm sure of it. Rene nods, indicating for me to put my school bag in the rusty tray of the ute.

I, without saying a word, decline. I take the passenger seat and nestle my bag between my feet on the floor of the cabin.

He tells me we're on our way to Brute's, whose property is right across the other side of the Depression.

The sky's grey now, with white dashes of cloud. Smoke haze around us from the wood fires and campfires and bonfires, and from people burning whatever else they don't want or what'll keep them warm. The paddocks are green, and some have purple streaks.

Weeds, Rene says. That's what happens when y'put somethin' that doesn't belong.

You send me a text that says: *let's play connect four*. Because I have a Samsung, the little images you've sent appear as tiny rectangular boxes. I don't want to reply saying I can't see the images. I reply saying: *I'm busy with Ren*. You send back: *Thats okay man, I get to see you soone!* You put another of those little images at the end of the text. The rectangle indecipherable — *what do you mean?*

I look up. We're driving past the matchstick tree farm. The trees in it don't look healthy, because they grow too tall too fast and thin and they drop branches, which Rene says means they're stressed. They chop 'em down each year and plant new saplings around the leftover stumps. Chop 'em down, cut 'em up, and make 'em into matchsticks.

Rene's ute doors are ajar. We've arrived. Because of the receding sunlight de-illuminating the Depression, the ute's weak headlights are turned onto the scene: a single ironbark tree and the two men, Rene and Brute, deciding the way the tree'll fall. Rene's shadow's long, stretches quite some way over the grassless ground under the ironbark's canopy. Brute's shadow, because of the angle he's standing at, is hugging his feet. Music comes out of the ute's cabin. From on the highest branch of the ironbark, a galah squawks and fissures the lyrics. It rustles its feathers — dishwater-grey and sunset-pink — as if scraps of cloth on a clothesline.

Buff and I lean against the ute's bonnet, between the headlights, so we don't disrupt the shining columns.

Where you, and even I, most of the time, scrounge money from home to buy lunch from the tuck shop at school, Buff Burrows always brings two salad and cold-meat sangas, minus beets and tomatoes because they make the bread soggy. He's the newer kid in town. His lunch is wrapped by his mother in cling wrap and accompanied by a Tupperware bottle with chocolate-flavoured protein powder, to which he adds water from the bubbler taps. He has a way of letting the hair above his top lip stay at a short length, allowing a few crumbs from his sangas to be suspended in his fine blonde fur. In the darkness, now, his skin is smooth, his muscle flatter, his stature more secret, quieter, insular than how he is at school. He puts one boot against the ute's grille; his foot slips and thuds back onto the earth. Buff's mouth's held how some people do when they're trying to extricate a piece of food, like a sharp piece of popcorn slicing delicate gum flesh.

I miss footy, he says.

It starts soon-ish.

Ish. Exactly, Bellos.

In this unspectacular evening, Rene Bello, a few paces away, begins hacking into the rough black trunk of the ironbark.

Between chops, Brute says he's sorry he can't help. It's a bad back an' the doc says I shouldn' do it.

I check my phone. No message from you.

Music's breaking inside me again: a lyric sparks a memory, like a votive candle. The flame casts light across Buff in cookery class at school last week. He'd sliced open his finger. The red blood mixed with the onion juice on the stainless blade, becoming iridescent, dripping down and soaking between the lines of the half-chopped onion on the bench. When Teacher got over to him, Buff said, It'll be right, with his finger in his mouth, sucking out his blood. His lips had smiled around the wound.

I walk to turn the radio off.

—

The only shire-wide public holiday rolls round — the Narioka Pastoral and Agricultural Show. Farmers from across the Depression come out of their fields to demonstrate their best wool, cattle, horses, produce. Woodcutters reveal the delicate furniture and feature pieces their rough hands have turned throughout the year. People of Narioka eat cake, sip tea, and gossip about the 'friends' they've not seen since last show. We go because we don't want to miss something. We sneak in through the back entrance so we don't have to pay the entry fee. We slip through the cattle pens and break out into sideshow alley.

Cecily's here, you say.

Right.

You mind if I catch up with her?

I do, but I say I don't; the sun strikes my eyes, and I can't really see where I'm going. I walk by myself. The eldest Drumanure kid is t-boning smaller kids on the bumper cars, Youarang across the way is trying to recruit people to be lifesavers, and those boys dart between the other rides, chasing each other, dacking unsuspecting passers-by and yelling, Faggot, between the tinny tunes of the Ferris wheel. A carny on a sideshow game waves me over. He's mid-teens, patchy facial hair, wears a red cap with the peak at the back; it's stained with sweat around the brim. His white t-shirt is grey, and his jeans stained, too. Tied round his waist is a leather money apron. As I get closer, he shoves his hands deep in the front pocket, as if plunging them down the front of his pants.

You here alone? the carny says.

I nod.

That's no good, he says as he moves his hand in his money apron. The coins jangle. Not even a mate?

I shake my head. He's meeting up with his girlfriend, I say.

Shit, the carny laughs. Don't blame yer, he says, leaning his elbows on the counter of his stall. Third wheelin's shitehouse. He rubs his chin. He shoves one hand deep into the leather money apron and pulls out a worn softball. He hands it to me as he says, Have a shot, it might change yer luck.

I've run out of coin, I lie to him. My pocket's clinging with coin. But he's squinting just as I am, and I don't know what he wants.

The carny looks despondent. He retracts the balls, dropping it back in his money apron, and puts his hands on his hips. He says, Ah, that's too bad. Tell yer what, he says, leaning forward, come back to me next year an' have a shot at me. He winks.

I leave, heading toward the exhibition sheds: Georges has entered some paintings, and Elmyra has entered her couture dresses. The exhibition sheds are two long barns clad in aluminium sheets. It's hot inside the first shed, a stale heat that I have to move through. In the first section, before the fashion displays, are cabinets with boiled fruitcakes and yo-yos and sponges I couldn't even get my mouth round. All the baked goods are sweating. Past these are flowers and then the handmade goods. In the back corner, propped up on a pedestal, is a mannequin draped with both the blue 'Champion Exhibit' and red 'Best Exhibit' sashes. Underneath these sashes is one of Elmyra's dresses: not made from a cookie-cutter pattern, the dress is constructed of two cuts of burgundy chiffon. There are no hard angles, only organic lines. The top sheath of chiffon is separated from the bottom section, which takes on its own personality, fulfilling the hips and flaring the hemline. I think it's made of chiffon and lace, but when I step closer I see that darker-burgundy, almost black, iridescent beads are set in the material and pull off the appearance of lace. Clusters of beads line the modestly cut neck, as well as the waist, where the seams have been sewn in a curved line to complement the overall design of the dress. She's called it 'Daisy', after *The Great Gatsby*.

You want to try it on?

I turn and find Elmyra standing behind me. I say, I don't think I have the hips.

She dismisses me with a pawing of her hand. You alone? she says, coming to stand beside me. She's facing her dress, looking at it as she speaks. There's a chicken-wire barrier in front of all the exhibits to stop the unwanted hands of children, or worse, adults touching the fine creations. It's through a few of these loops of chicken wire that Elmyra enlaces her fingers.

I say, Yair.

I thought you'd be with Grayson.

And you with Cecily.

She undoes her fingers from the wire and turns to me, then links arms.

I look round, seeing if anyone has noticed us. We pass out of the first shed and cross the short distance into the next. The first exhibits are sheep wool, already graded and awarded, before we come to the art at the far end. We slow, because we've traversed the entire tin shed and haven't found Georges's portraits, the ones I'd expected to see hanging.

What are you looking for? Elmyra says beside me.

Nothing, I say. *I'm looking for nothing. I'm thinking nothing. I'm laughing at nothing. I'm dreaming nothing. Speaking nothing. Am nothing.* I turn my head back to look at her then say, Nothing. Just looking.

That's not true, she says, I can see it in your eyes.

Ay?

What are you looking for?

I wanted to see Georges's pictures.

Pictures?

Yair, I say, the portraits he did of all of us. He was

going to enter them.

She laughs. Says, He just entered one painting, under the school's name. It's back down here. She unlinks herself, turns, and leads back to a spot we've already passed. She clasps her hands in front of her and nods to a broad canvas hanging above a fluffy pile of wool.

It's a wide crimson road and a night sky painted dark blue, the colour I've heard Georges call phthalo or something. The stars are pure-white dabs. To one side runs a barbed-wire fence, glistening with transparent raindrops. Ironbarks, their leaves fuzzy patches, stand illuminated, dully, by an orange-yellow moon breaking the horizon clouds. The painting's won Champion Exhibit and Best Exhibit, the same as Elmyra's dress.

Standing before Georges's art, I feel like I know him. Where do you think he is? I say.

Probably at home—

Why?

She laughs. He's probably as embarrassed his thoughts have been emblazoned on a wall as mine have on a mannequin.

Then why aren't you hiding at home like he is?

It's only a month or two after this that the school holidays begin. Summer, its searing whiteness and brittle calamity, dehydrates the Depression. The cicadas sing. I get a text from you at a quarter past noon.

We goin' campen?

Of course.

Sleeping beside someone: I've never done it.

Elmyra's old man an' I used t' top an' tail when we were your age, Rene says as he lays out two pillows. One at the bottom for me, and the other, at the top of the bed, meant for you.

I look at your pillow and wonder why we can't sleep side by side, like Rene does with Elba. I say, Won't my feet get in his face?

Rene stands up after flattening the sheets. Just hope he doesn't have funguses growing.

It's not the fungus I'm worrying about.

Rene tells me to fill in time.

He'll be here soon, I say.

Not till after four, bud, says Rene.

So there I go, again: I do jobs on Rene's farm. Whenever I do this, I try to complete them as best I can. But I'm always distracted. By things such as how the land formed a kazillion years ago — long before some cocksure defined what's natural and what's not, and definitely long before the buildings in town were erected or the man-made bushlands around the Lake were established. I like to imagine how the earth ripped itself apart, swallowed the pastoral plains of the Depression and plunged it into an antiquity of generational quicksand. In my mind, I make the woman engineer who planned and built not only Narioka but also the only road, zigzagging up the cliffs and over to the higher Plain, a hero holding up a trophy. And I wonder if an asteroid collided with Earth the second I was born, and if that, somehow, would make me a creation of this geography.

When I get back to the house, you're standing at the front door with dishelmed hair, maybe just-woken, and smiling as if you've injected liquid happiness: a potion of clear sunlight, the motion of butterflies and not the butterflies themselves, and every note of laughter to have ever escaped. Even the bad tones of laughter, like when Elmyra told us how her cat had climbed under the bonnet of her mother's car and fallen asleep on the engine, and been fried there when she'd started it. They hadn't known about it until it'd begun to smoke from under the bonnet. An old lady in the street, El had told me with a smile, had said they'd best be checking the water. Then, without a smile, she said how her mother'd plied the steaming body from the engine and dumped it in the footpath bin, saying they didn't need the fucken stupid thing anyway. One less mouth to feed.

At dinner, you pull the peas away from the mash with the fine prongs of your fork. While you do it, you tell me about the time you broke into the public swimming pool and say, We should do it, too.

One day, I reply.

And you say, One day will get away from you.

By and by, we sneak a swig of port or marsala or some equal repugnance; by and by, we shower and you tell me to get out from under the water and you turn it up real hot, cut the cold, so we're in a sauna or steam room, and it's cool because the white mist is rising up and your immoderate laugh is that very steam; by and by, the movie you brought over (*Bad Boy Bubby*) finishes and Rene, tired-eyes, says bed; and, by and by, we're side by side, none of that top-and-tail crap.

In the morning, you turn to me and say, We're wild today, no need for clothes and towels and shit.

We pushbike toward the Lake without our helmets on. Going fast, we both have speed-wobbles as we pass the path to school and head around the bend where the bush around the Lake begins. The crushed stone crunches as the rubber touches it, and we scream and yell, Fuck you, fucken cunts, and the wind from our speed shakes the sound through the green leaves above, a noise that makes me smile. I close my eyes. My front wheel enters a cleft in the road. Jars. Shimmies. Flips. I zoom over the handlebars into a weedy table drain. I roll through brittle grass. You skid to a stop. I make a guttural sound as I come to a halt.

I can't tell if you're bending over because of the angle the drain's at or because of your laughter. You're laughing hard: no noise comes out, and your face is red, and you drop to the ground beside me, and your hands wrap around your stomach.

Get the fuck up, I say.

We pull up near some small eucalypts on the edge of the Lake. Their roots break past the bank and twist into the water.

Carn, let's get this fucker out. You throw the bundled tent on the ground. It tumbles toward the water and you run after it to stop it.

I place the fishing rods against a tree.

The sunlight drops. Bull ants (*Myrmecia gulosa*) crawl at our feet. Cockatoos roost. I cast the fishing line.

You spit on the ground and say, How's the new kid?

I open my mouth. Phlegm catches. I cough and then say, Buff?

Buff, he calls himself. Came from the city. Bloody wanker.

You don't know him.

Anyone wearing sunnies on their first day is a wanker, and who introduces themself with a nickname?

I reel in and cast again.

What's Georges think? you say.

He doesn't say much about anything.

He's a top bloke. You should give him a shot, and I don't mean pickin' him on the school footy team. You pat your pockets. Did you bring ciggies?

I shake my head and say, Georges told me he doesn't like footy.

Yair, when? Footy's like one of the biggest things for you, Markus.

Yair whatever, Gray, he said it. And footy's not a big thing for me, it's just Rene trying to be young again through me.

You climb inside the tent. When you come back out, you've already lit up. I think you should give Georges a chance, Markus. The kid's good, an' bloody brilliant at drawing.

I scratch my nose. What makes him a good bloke?

You sit down and hint that he's more like me.

What's that mean?

He's just, I dunno, like you, and I reckon you'd hit it off. Ask him. You'll know.

I don't answer. I reel in and cast again. The sinker plods before the current drags the line away. I flick the bail over and rest the rod between my legs.

We make a fire and stretch across the dirt. I've given up on fish.

The sky twinkles with stars.

You, through a mouthful of biscuit, ask me, What are y'gunna do when school finishes, like when it's over?

Dunno. You?

Mm, I wanna go to the conservatorium in the city. Gunna shove it up the arse-munchers. You laugh. Mum can't afford that, but. I'll stay around here, might get a giggin' job at one of the pubs.

With a band?

You don't answer.

The fire's embers crack.

Markus.

Yair?

It'd be nice to get outta here.

I sniff.

Just a thought, you say.

It's absurd how much I need you, even though I know that needing you is bad for me. You ask me, What's ticking in that head of yours?

The stars.

You push your chin back and gaze to the heavens. You say, There's gotta be more than a trillion.

Kazillion, I say.

Ha! That's a bit much.

What do you mean?

There's heaps, but a kazillion's a bit much.

Overwhelming?

You agree.

Why would too many be overwhelming? I say.

I don't even know where the fuck to look, you say.

I point to one among others. That one.

I'm not sure you're looking at the right one. And you say you don't know.

The one that stands out.

You say, The moon?

I shake my head.

Why not? It's the biggest and brightest.

Don't you remember, Teacher said it reflects the light of the sun; it's fake. What would you choose?

You point over the top of my face. That one, the one that gets away before the night's done, an' rises again with the sun.

Crickets and cicadas buzz.

You say, it's too hot to sleep in clothes.

We strip to our undies and then to nakedness. Hang our clothes on a low tree branch. Under the moonlight, our skins are silver.

You run down to and dive under the water. Bubbles. You come up for air. Coming in, Markus? Or gunna stand there starkers? You spray the drips off your lips. You'll be fine once you get in.

My body splashes, waves eat at the undercut ridge on the bank. When I come up for air, the night's much colder. I don't want to leave. I can't see you. Oi, cunt! I call. My feet swivel in the sludge at the bottom.

Your voice replies from the bank.

The fuck? The waterline bobs around my diaphragm.

You wipe your pearl skin and pull your undies on. It was just to cool down, Markus.

I could yell and lie back and float and gaze past the dark leaves of the trees, gaze up into the deep, dark, exposed universe. Laugh and get that flock of bloody cockatoos awake and squawking. Your voice, and the way you turn and duck inside the tent, draws me out.

You're lying on top of your sleeping bag. Your hands behind your head. You're looking at the tent's canopy.

I lay on my own sleeping bag. The cotton from my undies sticks to my groin. I avoid unpicking it.

Two-man tents are really for a single person, you say.

I listen to the noises outside.

You roll onto your shoulder.

We're facing each other.

Buff'll be here tomorrow night, you say. And for now your eyes sink and I look back to those brown smiling eyes. You breathe as older boys do when they turn into men. You smell of oranges and cut grass, a scent that lingers from when we'd eaten stolen oranges before we rode out here.

You're right about two-man tents, I say.

The school holidays aren't always so full of people. Some days, Myf Warhurst is the only person to lunch with me. In the background, on the radio, her voice heavy and used to the frequency. Elmyra told me that female radio presenters are told to lower the tone of their voices so they're not whiney-high and sound more masculine. Myf leaves me out of the conversation. There's a song she plays that invites me to sing along.

I lie on the couch after lunchtime and read a book about Rimbaud's lost voyage to Java. I mouth the words I know from the radio. I don't take in a word of the book. Later, there's a thunderstorm. Rain falls heavy and the thunder settles down someplace in the room with me, grumbling around the space I'm not occupying. Rimbaud remains elusive.

I get a message from you asking if I sent you anything.

I read it a few times. Perhaps this message was meant for someone else. I send back: *Yep I sent a message earlier but mightn't have had enough service.*

You don't reply.

In my bedroom, I undress to nakedness. Built-up tension and the horniness of a fifteen-year-old combine with a genuine sense of exploration, as if discovering virgin lands. I masturbate as the summer storm outside asserts its presence over the Depression.

When I'm laying spent on my bed, you text me a silly excuse for not replying earlier; another excuse I try to ignore. You tell me you were *mowing the lawns*, and I doubt this because it's storming outside. You say: *We'll make plans at the back of the rail yard.*

We go.

We smoke and cough and shiver, shielding our bodies from the rain. Huddling against the grain shed, I look across to the silo. Its smooth walls melt with the rainwater. From the side of the grain store, you dart out of shelter. Your foot lands on the rusted rail tracks cutting through the middle of the yard. You suspend the moment before your knee springs out, and your body leaps over and toward the silo. You're like a ballet dancer, in control of every muscle. You put your hands against the tower to stop your momentum.

You're ducking from the rain as if ducking from a hurtling stone. You yell, Carn.

I butt out the cigarette, half-smoked, and rush through the increasing rain. I trip on the rail tracks. I get beside you beneath the silo's tiny, inset door.

Wanna go up, you say, *mi compañero*? Close and muggy, your breath lands against my neck.

I could kiss you. You're not even looking at me.

You're running your fingers over the hinges of the door.

I blink in the rain, which slants under the cover and lands about my face.

You can't sit at home forever, Markus, making plans for things you say you're gunna do an' never do. You stand up and push me aside. You get at the door handle. Jig it and, after having to put your foot against the wall, you pull ajar the door.

Dust comes out and is pattered away by rain.

Follow me.

The door was welded shut for a reason, I say.

Shitty welder if ever — faaark, Markus.

It's about to fall over, I say, gazing up the side of the silo. The clouds swirling make its walls seem not to be melting but to be descending over us.

Trust me, you say.

I say, where've I heard that before?

Hasn't failed you yet? You wink and punch my shoulder.

Inside is cold. Rubbing my skin makes no difference. The windows, of which there're six, run vertically up the central column of the silo. Beyond those walls, the siren of an ambulance yawns. In here smells like rat (*Rattus*) and pigeon (*Ocyphaps lophotes*). The latter coo down at us, perhaps commenting on our appearance, as if we've disrupted an important meeting.

I think the ladder'll break from rust, I say.

But you climb, regardless of the rust, up that steel ladder inside, pulling yourself to the top of the silo. I stay down on the ground, minding my feet in the piles of pigeon shit, looking up. I call out, I'll catch you if you fall.

Afterward, we take our pushies down the Lake, take our pushies and nothing more. The day's dying. There's a faraway pinhead light in the sky, gleaming over the rim of the cliffs. Grey cloud orbits it. Unchaseable.

Venus, you say putting your back brakes on. The rubber wheel snakes along the dirt.

Bull.

See? It's not twinkling, means the light off it is

reflected, means it's not a star — you told me that.

We dismount: for now, rooted to the valley's floor. Our bikes topple. The section of the Lake we choose might be said to be near town. We say it's enough away to make as much noise as we can, and still the Depression will eat up our existence. I could die here, because only the hardest people leave the security of the Depression. Near the edge where we pull up is a eucalypt. It's bare and could be dead. It stands as if waiting in the evening for a lover to call.

I climb. Grainy bark presses at the palms of my hands and knocks against my kneecaps. Bare toes scratch at the trunk and find a way to stable footing. The babbling water makes me think of you. I call out, Coming up? My voice doesn't echo; it speeds out over the landscape and becomes lost somewhere near the edge of town. As it does, I continue stretching my eyes upward. With my young chest pushing out, I draw my body further into the tangle of twigs. I'm cheerful. I call again, Come on up.

Your voice denies anything outside of you. I hear it loudly say, Little boys climb trees. It deflects off the environment and becomes intimate, like a thought.

This is when the Lake fills. Unexpectedly, the water authorities release excess water into the system. It falls over the lip of the cliffs and into the Lake. No one, even those in the Mayday Hills old people's home, has seen this before. At lunchtimes, the nurses bring the elderly out to the shoreline. Their wheelchairs and walking frames catch in the sand and make them laugh. The water continues falling, muddies, and begins rising as a slush creeps onto the shores of the Lake. Sun excites the surface.

Rene takes me fishing.

Fish? I ask. Grayson and I caught nothing the other day in the creek.

Don't be silly, the creek has nothin' in it. The fish come down from upstream, he says. You two don't know nothin'.

We take two rods and an esky, with beer for me and Coke for Rene.

Elba worries about me drinking young.

Rene says, You have to learn how to handle yer grog.

Sky-blue space above us, and a slight breeze. A radio sings. Underneath this sound is the splashing of the waterfall to the south, where what the Plain above doesn't want pours down into the Depression. Bird life joins it: pelicans (*Pelecanus conspicillatus*) shift across the surface, spoonbills (*Platalea regia*) and cormorants (*Phalacrocorax sulcirostris*).

As I finish placing my fold-out chair, I turn and see Elmyra running toward us.

She's bikinied and has a large-brimmed floppy sunhat and wide Monroe shades. She hugs me, and I smell an earthen scent and sunscreen. Letting her go, I ask where she's set up. She points back to the way she'd run from.

It smells like sewage, she says. She gestures to the waterfall.

Smaller kids play under its crashing wall, the curtain breaking and splintering off their bodies. Rene, Elmyra, and I stare at the water. A speedboat zips past near the middle, its spray like mercury. The boat recedes, and the sound following it is the distant hush of the waterfall.

Rene says, Goin' in?

I swish some flies from my face.

Ya better, he says. Doesn't fill often. Not even ya granddad ever saw any in it.

Elba calls out.

Rene heads up shore and Elmyra runs away, shouting over her shoulder that she'll come back after lunch.

I assess the depth I could plunge to. The streaks of white between the grey will rip open and swallow the sky; those streaks are just ripples on the surface with sunlight reflecting at different angles. Whatever. The heat's settled into my bones and my legs. I look back to Rene and Elba. She has a hand on her hip and the other flipping around in front of her. I remove my thongs. Sandy dirt burns my feet. I try to stand for as long as I can, to withstand the pain. I run down to the water after no more than ten or twelve seconds. Knee-deep, not waist, I stand in the cold water. Crossing my arms over my chest as if the day's freezing and not 43°C, I establish a perfect footy pose. Season's training starts soon; Rene's signed me up, says he reckons I'll make a ripping forward pocket. It's not my thing, but no one listens. I stare past the flotilla with the other boys my age jumping from its edge. Through the boys' laughter and the shouts of *fucken faggot*, *pussy*, and *sunken cunt*, I hear a constant hush. At this year's camp, back in early April, you were some other kind of island on your knees. Today, I look back at the nearby water tower that everyone pretends is the lighthouse from *Round The Twist*. I wish I'd never sighted you.

The Lake continues filling, and the sewage-smelling water swells. Overnight, water lifts debris and fills the Depression. The water spreads dark and cold under the moonlight and bursts from the tributary creek, which cuts Narioka in two, and rises between the buildings, deadening any light. Puts out what's been put up. By dawn, there is nothing except water and debris. When the flood recedes from the useless sandbag walls, which let most of the water through, it leaves a dirty watermark, and mould, and other icky things that the SES clear. The roads are muck. A car speeding at midnight slips into a table drain. Single fatality. Many sick with what Doctor says is stress. They lie in bed awaiting safety. In time, the flood becomes a memory instead of a presence. The Lake retracts to a manageable level. Its source, the waterfall, is gone.

I wasn't in town at the time, and the flood that swelled submerged Narioka alone. It so happens that within the Depression there's a smaller geographical depression, a 'ditch' if you will, inside which Narioka's built. When the water rose, the water, naturally, flowed and filled the ditch. When they decided to build the town there, a woman engineer had said not to because of this geographical flaw. A bunch of unqualified people said one thing, and she alone said another thing. She had her right to have her view expressed, but, based on majority, did not have the right to be given the same amount of time or space as the unqualified bunch. All she had built at her initial town-site, as if to please her, was a small, steeple-less and stained-glassless church. And I didn't quite understand how frustrated she might have been until I saw the town underwater, which is why I enjoyed it when Rene drove me to the edge of town to see it.

Soon after, it changes season. Colder, greener. They've cleaned up town enough in time for us to go back to school.

Teacher says, When you kick a football, the ball accelerates toward the ground at a constant speed. The ball seems to speed as it leaves your foot and seems to slow when it's in the air, before it seems to speed again as it drops back to the Earth.

To prove the point, I have to plot on a graph the football that Buff'll kick. The y-axis is to be vertical speed, and the x-axis is to be time.

I sit at the back of the class as Teacher speaks. I jab a compass into my thigh, like on a sewing machine.

Teacher says, Mark, are you going to do it?

It's pointless, I say. It proves that you never make progress.

Ah, Teacher says, there's something to describe that. Teacher introduces us to imaginary numbers. They call imaginary numbers 'i'. Calculating with i is the mathematical equivalent of believing in fairies or God. i is abstract and useful in concrete ways: it can be used to work out living things like the nautilus or eucalypts, or working things like bridges and towers and noises, or invisible things like radio waves and dark matter drifting about, otherwise unknown.

Whatever.

Night falls. Silent darkness.

From the clouds that were pointed at during the day, a light snow falls: champagne powder on the fields and houses and streets and cows and sheep and cars. The Lake begins to freeze from the edges. The brown-green water crystallises and solidifies into a thick bed of ice.

I don't see the snowfall, only the snow.

The methane-sewage smell dissipates. Everything — well, the atmosphere at least — becomes crisp and clean. Almost pure.

When I wake, I walk down to the open-plan area.

Rene, with a coffee in his hand and toast crumbs at the corners of his lips, calls me over.

We have a new prime minister. Went to bed with one and wake to have another: the killing season executed in the dead of night. Those tremors of the capital won't reach us here. We're over the Great Divide and exist only theoretically.

We're a safe seat, Rene says. Always have and always will be. Everyone knows safe seats don't get funding.

The next news story is about same-sex marriage: the new overlord declares that any member who doesn't toe the party line will be sacked.

Rene says, That's unconstitutional, undemocratic.

What is?

Sackin' someone f'not believin' what y'tell 'em to.

But can't the prime minister do whatever?

No, Markus, god no. We're not America.

I keep quiet because I don't quite understand; I think of 'gotten'. And of hypocrisy.

Elba says, In Australia we vote for a party, not for a leader. The party choose their leader and, as we've seen, the party can also change leaders.

Rene says, The party doesn't care what voters will think of it.

They've their cushy jobs and nice retirement funds, Elba says.

I ask, Why can't the party believe what they want?

Neither of them answer me.

Elmyra calls and says she's going ice-skating. Want to

come? She says she's sitting beside the Lake's edge and can see there's a sprinkling over the diamond-hard crust, which, under the impromptu lighting, looks like golden fairy dust.

I say, I don't have ice skates. She laughs. Silly, she says, Mr Burrows is renting them out to people.

I can see her wearing her indigo-coloured fluffy-puffy winter jacket and pale-denim skinny jeans, sitting idle on a seat with black ice skates laced to her feet. Cecily, she says, left moments before I arrived. It's sometime after twilight: après-ski. She skates anyway, alone: the Lady of the Lake. I sit on the edge, and she looks like a cabbage butterfly (*Pieris rapae*), but more graceful because she's conscious of her aim. We get hot chocolate and she, with a pastel-orange tipped finger, puts a bit of froth on my nose. I try to lick it off. We laugh.

She says, as I'm walking her back to her house, Did you hear what happened to Georges after school?

I shake my head.

Those boys jumped him.

What?

Black eyes, blood all over the road — or so Buff told me. She nods long and slow, deep in her hot chocolate. He's okay, if you're wondering.

I shake my head. Why'd they do it?

She doesn't reply.

Despite this, despite everything, so many of us rarely reply with the reply someone needs the most. Or perhaps our replies escape us, or come to us after the fact, so neither of us is at fault. A fault like the Depression our shire's built in. At the time, I didn't consider faults to be character weaknesses or impairing physical perfection. It's your fault, Elba used to screech at Rene. I.e., you are being discontinuous, you are impairing physical perfection, you are my weakness. I wonder if she's given as much thought to the creation of the Depression as I have. Because actions can't be right or wrong; the morality of them lies in the outcome, which depends on how each action is taken.

Like Elmyra, when we looked at her mother's atlas, would say, It's not fixed and doesn't determine the direction we should take. She'd be following the lines of some mountainous ridge, trying to find a pathway through. I think she knew how I felt about you and that was her way of saying something, of navigating the subject, so to speak. But her silence, her saying nothing now, is worse than her saying everything I ever wanted to hear from her. Specifically *I know and it's okay.*

I get on my motorbike. I could drop by yours and chill. When I come to the turn for your place, the motorbike keeps going, heading back to Rene's.

Elba's at the table in the dining room. The telly in the lounge has a repeat of *The Great Outdoors* episode dedicated to Spain.

I nod at her.

She giggles. How was skating? Bet you only do that

once in a lifetime.

I say, It was fine. I look at the pamphlets for Barcelona and maps for Santiago. I ask her about her day.

She looks away from me, saying something about great things are coming.

Rene's growing hemlock at the same time as he grows root vegetables. He wakes me early one morning on the weekend, telling me to come and help.

I always help, I growl.

That's 'cause yer me son, he chuckles.

But it's five in the morning, I moan, pulling the doona back over my head.

Early bird, he says and rips the doona away.

So I dress in some old clothes and meet him in the veggie patches just outside the back door.

Out back, he hands me a seedling tray and says, Be careful.

Why?

Hemlock — *Conium maculatum*, he says, family *Umbelliferae*. He flicks his free hand backward to one of the nearby garden beds. Says, Same as parsley, fennel, parsnip an' carrot. Umbelliferous plants have an acrid juice, a narcotic. Rene drags the final word out as if he's enjoying it. He snaps the stem of one of the seedlings and shows me the sap seeping out and bulging, waiting to burst at the tip. Sticky-white.

I think of the border of a shore, like the edge of a mind. An invisibly stitched shoreline where water washes up, lapping at the edge, inviting yet indifferent. Its white foam pushing up the shore, left there when the body of liquid retreats.

Every part of hemlock, Rene says, 'specially the leaves, have oily alkaloids, poison. A few drops kill an animal.

I place the tray of seedlings down on the ground and wipe my hands on my trackies. When I speak, a plume of white escapes from my mouth. I say, Why are you growing it then?

Might not be a native, Rene says, but some say it keeps the pests away. He goes on digging holes, making me take out a seedling at a time from the tray for him to put into the holes.

When we're done, he tells me we need firewood.

I tell him Elmyra's coming. She'd said on the phone, I'm trying to be caring. It has something to do with her thinking I'm not myself. I am confusion. And I'm not just talking about sexual, identity, hormonal or teenage confusion. That shit's normal. Angst. Everyone has it. I mean confusion about you. Where are you; what are you; who are you? And why do I feel like you are my anchor? I hear you inside me, like taking a seashell to my ear.

Rene shrugs and says, Do it before she gets here.

I get on my motorbike, rev and ride out and along the

track to a far paddock. My bike zips through the sweeping plains grass. I come up to the fallen tree. I'd felled it back in the midsummer, and now, as I approach its remains, it is a bare black streak swarmed by yellow grass. Get some more wood, I tell myself, keep the fires burning, it's getting cold, winter's coming. These are excuses.

Thunk.

I lift the maul, hack the hollow-sounding bark again, and work through to the trunk, working from where I'd last cut. The arching, twisted limb creaks. It's as if I've known this tree my entire life; as if I've helped plant it, as if I've watched it grow over the years and as if, because of my involvement, I've been made to clean up its leftovers. This tree is another of the thousands dotted through the shire. The maul's sound makes me remember. I don't want to. I can't help it. Images I've suppressed shift around inside my head and allow a perspective to arrive.

Thunk.

It was April.

Elmyra chooses a classroom at school. We'll do silent study, she giggles, rolls her eyes and leads into a vacant room along the veranda. She speaks about nothing I find interesting. I follow her because I have yet to find someone closer to follow. After Elmyra settles into her chair, a group of boys my age come along and stand out on the veranda.

Thunk.

I can't name them except one. I know your name, for

sure. Can-could-will-had always put a face and a body and a smile and voice to your name. To you. Even when you're not near. It's not that I do not know the other boys. I do. I've never been interested in the other boys. I remember Elmyra. I say to her, What d'you think they've planned?

She turns around. Remains quiet.

Thunk.

From within the art room, the window captures you like a frame from a movie — a silent movie. What proves you're alive are your actions. The sun lines your body and beams brighter in the scruffy, dark-honey hair wisping across your forehead and up to the right. The rest of your hair, on top, uncurls in delicate tufts. Both your hands clutch your school shirt at your hips; the material stretches taut across your back. You flex your elbows as if trying to meet them behind you, not too extreme, gentle-like, and this makes your shirt tight over your stomach and chest. It defines your torso, as if no shirt is clothing your body at all. You squint when you laugh and bend forward, lifting one leg about a foot off the ground. You keep the rest intact.

Thunk.

He's wanting a party, Elmyra's quiet voice says in a steady tone.

Thunk.

I've often contemplated the image of Elmyra as she sat upon her hands when I said, I'll always go to a party of his.

IV.

Eighteen

On the night of Markus's eighteenth birthday, Grayson rolls his eyes when Buff arrives. It's nine o'clock and hot, and Buff's only wearing a pair of yellow shorts. He says he's meant to be a lifeguard. The shorts are tight and stick to his thighs: he looks more like Rocky Horror. It was Elmyra's idea to have it dress up, because her party's out on a farm tomorrow night, and they can't wear costumes then because they'll get dirty. She's Marilyn from when she sang (i.e., the real Marilyn) 'Happy Birthday' to Mr President. Markus takes her white-fur coat and hangs it up for her. Grayson's a Greek god. He says, It was my mother's idea, I forget who the god is. The toga he's wearing seems breezy. He has what Markus guesses is a wreath of leaves on his head, which is made of mistletoe he's probably stripped out of a eucalypt tree. Mistletoe — a parasitic plant — spreads when a bird eats its seeds and shits them out on the branches of other trees. It looks more like a thorny tangle of weeds.

Rene comes over with a cake. Markus laughs out his nose and snuffs the candles prematurely. Markus sees Gray's face across the table, somewhat more distant than he'd like him to be. Distant and dramatic in the dim light that the now re-lit candles are casting. They're singing happy birthday. Elmyra uses a stubby in place of a microphone. Grayson breaks the tune when he sneezes.

After, everyone starts the piss-up.

Markus is standing around the side of the house, taking a leak.

Grayson slaps him on his shoulder.

Markus pisses on his own feet and feels it, because he's dressed as Aquaman and wearing green thongs.

Carn, Gray says.

They slip further around the corner of the house toward the front. There are no obvious party-ers. Grayson pulls him down behind the bonnet of someone's car. Points across it. Underneath the orange geraniums Rene's bordered with red bricks, there are two figures. Markus turns to Gray, who, with a rounded and warm palm, turns Markus's head back to the figures. The moon's light is broken by the trees overhead. Maybe one of the figures is a shirtless man, maybe the other a blonde-haired woman.

What are they doing? Markus whispers.

Grayson flicks his hand against Markus's shoulder

and says, Gardening. He laughs quietly. Carn. He ducks and weaves between the cars and Markus follows, trying to keep up.

Markus wants to say, *Slow down so I can follow*. Out on the road into town, the sky is unimpeded by the leaves of trees. The moonlight sprinkles. Grayson's marble-white toga is bold as he walks. Markus ditches his thongs in a table drain because they're giving him blisters between his toes. Cool dirt on his bare feet. Markus pulls up the Aquaman mask he made and lets it rest against the top of his head.

Gray.

Yair?

But Markus kinda doesn't wanna ask where they're going. He says instead, How many stars d'you think there are?

Grayson doesn't answer for a bit. We've had this conversation, he says.

Yair, well, I wanna know what you think now.

Nothin' different.

Truth is, Markus can't remember what *mi compañero* had said all those years ago.

Their feet on the sandy track crunch out of time. Up ahead, a dim glow from the lights in town.

Markus quickens to catch up. He's a little disappointed. Where are we going?

But Grayson shushes him.

The boys head by the road through the drying-out land toward Narioka. In the dark, the cliffs are indiscernible, and they could very well be on a vast plain that stretches forever without any borders. The hydrophobic-red dirt gathers from a crumble into pavement and then to bitumen. The main road. And the spiny strands of grasses and weeds, dead or dying and yellowish-grey, bind around each other to form the faux gold-rush buildings. Down Melville Street, past the newsagents, chemist, and past where, in the bright daylight, the young vagrants will smoke rolled cigarettes, drink Red Bull, and whack their children out front of the Chicken Ranch. Tonight, the footpaths are caverns of emptiness. The boys come to the public swimming pool.

Near the back of the complex, Grayson lifts a corner of the cyclone-wire fence. Big enough for a superhero, he says as Markus crawls underneath.

And a Greek god, Markus replies.

Grayson enters unaided, and as he stands up, he says, You told me there's no such thing as gods or goddesses. He de-togas. He's in his underwear and sprints toward the water, leaps and dives into the pool. He's standing in its mid-section, where he turns and yells back to Markus, You comin' in?

Acknowledgements

Many thanks to Marika for her careful and considered editing on this book, as well as to the Scribe Publications team.

Thank you also to the following people for your much needed and welcomed support: Mum, Guy, Deni, Grace, and my friends from RMIT.